"Surprised to see you back here," Sam said.

"Surprised? Why?"

"You were in such a rush to leave. I'm pretty sure there's still tire marks outside the Homestead Pass Community Church."

"I sent you a letter. I apologized." She bit her lip and narrowed her eyes. In defense or concern?

His jaw tightened. "Yep. You sent me a letter."

"Is that why you're here? To give me a piece of your mind?"

"Not exactly." This was about business. "I'd like a minute of your time to discuss the contract."

Liv exhaled sharply, then stared at him long and hard. "Why? Didn't you get my check?"

"I did." Sam refused to give her an inch.

Once again, the silence stretched.

"Okay, fine," Liv said. "You want to talk. We can talk." Clearly, not happy.

That made two of them.

Yep, they were going to talk. He'd waited too many long years for this reunion, and he had plenty to say, including half a dozen good reasons why she shouldn't rent his building.

Tina Radcliffe has been dreaming and scribbling for years. Originally from Western New York, she left home for a tour of duty with the US Army Security Agency stationed in Augsburg, Germany, and ended up in Tulsa, Oklahoma. Her past careers include certified oncology RN, library cataloger and pharmacy clerk. She recently moved from Denver, Colorado, to the Phoenix, Arizona, area, where she writes heartwarming and fun inspirational romance.

Books by Tina Radcliffe

Love Inspired

Lazy M Ranch

The Baby Inheritance
The Cowboy Bargain

Hearts of Oklahoma

Finding the Road Home
Ready to Trust
His Holiday Prayer
The Cowgirl's Sacrifice

Big Heart Ranch

Claiming Her Cowboy
Falling for the Cowgirl
Christmas with the Cowboy
Her Last Chance Cowboy

Love Inspired Suspense

Sabotaged Mission

Visit the Author Profile page
at LoveInspired.com for more titles.

The Cowboy Bargain

Tina Radcliffe

LOVE INSPIRED

INSPIRATIONAL ROMANCE

LOVE INSPIRED®
INSPIRATIONAL ROMANCE

ISBN-13: 978-1-335-41759-6

The Cowboy Bargain

Recycling programs
for this product may
not exist in your area.

Love Inspired
22 Adelaide St. West, 41st Floor
Toronto, Ontario M5H 4E3, Canada
www.LoveInspired.com

Printed in U.S.A.

And be ye kind one to another, tenderhearted,
forgiving one another, even as God
for Christ's sake hath forgiven you.
—*Ephesians* 4:32

Grazie di cuore (heartfelt thanks) to my Italian grandmothers, Mary Barreca and Anna Testa, who immigrated to the States from Sicily and Naples. They gave me unconditional love and many tasty hours in their kitchens.

Thank you to Tom at Chino Woodcraft for keeping my woodworking terminology accurate—visit chinowoodcraft.com. A special thank-you goes out to my friend and chef Robyn S. for her ideas as well.

I am blessed and thankful to have the prayers and support of the Oklahoma Wranglers, my reader team, who made this book possible.

A final thanks to my agent Jessica Alvarez and my editor Katie Gowrie. Never underestimate the power of a savvy woman in your corner.

Chapter One

"It's not my fault."

"What isn't your fault, Gramps?" Sam Morgan yanked off his tie and stared at his grandfather. Only five minutes ago, he'd driven past the welcoming Lazy M Ranch sign, relieved to be back in Homestead Pass, Oklahoma, and its down-home beauty after a week in Vegas. Now he wasn't so sure.

"I rented out that shop space downtown," Gus Morgan said.

"Thanks. I appreciate you handling that while I was gone." He frowned at the worried expression on his grandfather's face. "So, what's the problem?"

"I rented it to Olivia."

"What?" Sam did a double take. Familiar dread rose as he processed the mention of his ex-fiancée. Olivia Moretti, the woman who'd practically left him at the altar and humiliated him in front of the entire town.

His grandfather pulled off his Stetson and then slapped it back on his head. "How was I supposed to know that OMM Enterprises was Olivia Moretti? The lawyer fella never let on."

"Liv is back in Homestead Pass?" Sam worked to wrap his head around the information.

"From what I hear, she's been here on and off, checking on her father's health."

On and off? Well, she'd done an excellent job of staying off his radar. In the last five years, he hadn't even seen the back of her head in church on Sunday. Homestead Pass wasn't big like Elk City down the road, yet somehow she'd managed to avoid him. He wasn't sure if he should be glad or annoyed. Right now, annoyance held the upper hand.

"Yep. Decided to stay this time." The

elder cowboy rubbed the gray shadow of whiskers on his face. "She's got a plan for a farm-to-table restaurant downtown. I had to look up what that means, by the way."

"In my building?" Sam's brain short-circuited at the words. At the same time, synapses fired off warning bells, whistles and a dozen questions.

"Yep." Gramps gave a slow shake of his head as the sharp blue eyes assessed Sam for a reaction.

"Has she signed the contract yet?"

"Uh-huh, and I countersigned."

A contract signed by Liv and Sam's designated agent, Gus Morgan. All more than three days ago. *Perfect.*

Sam grumbled under his breath and barely refrained from commenting. He was tired and cranky and probably should have headed to his own house on the ranch, but the thought of the ranch housekeeper's baked goods had enticed him to the Lazy M Ranch house. Bess Lowder was one of the best cooks around and they were blessed to have her employed at the Morgan homestead.

Sam glanced around the spacious kitchen of his childhood, sniffing the air. The aroma of yeast, butter and cinnamon teased his senses. "Did Bess make cinnamon rolls today?"

"Sure, she did. And I happen to know that she saved an entire pan for you to take home. I just don't know where. She hides them from me."

"As she should. Where is Bess anyhow?"

"In the garden, planting."

Sam took a step toward the hall leading to the back door.

"Maybe you should hear the rest of the news before you head outside."

A shiver raced over Sam as he slowly turned back. "The rest of the news?"

His grandfather's blue eyes were wary now. "Miss Olivia rented both units in the building."

"Gramps." A dull ache throbbed at Sam's temples.

"I know you were tossing around the idea of using the other space, but her lawyer insisted on both shops or nothing at all. Got him to sweeten the deal by agreeing to pay for twelve months' rent upfront. I figured even you wouldn't turn that down." Gus Morgan cocked his head. "What were your plans for the other space anyhow?"

"Handcrafted fine wood products by Samuel J. Morgan. I told you that the last time you asked." Sam had worn many hats in his life—bronc buster, bulldogger, ranch hand, and now, the ranch accountant. None gave him the satisfaction that working with his hands did.

"Huh. I don't seem to recall that discussion." Gramps paused. "You mean you're gonna sell those things you make?"

"Those things I make?" Sam tamped down his frustration. "You're referring to the planter boxes, trays, cutting boards and signs?" He'd built up quite an inventory over the years and had ideas for more. If only there were more hours in the day.

"Weren't you making birdhouses?" Gramps cocked his head.

"I've advanced some since the last time you visited the workshop." Sam shook his head and eyed his grandfather.

"Hmm. So you're thinking about selling your crafts." Gus shrugged. "Guess I didn't realize it was anything but a hobby."

"It's not a hobby." Sam shook his head. Why was it so difficult to get his family to take his woodworking seriously?

Jesus was a carpenter. Had his family given him grief too?

His grandfather raised his hands. "Don't take offense. You already have two jobs, so I just figured—"

"It's okay, Gramps." Sam released a breath. "So, tell me. At what point did you realize it was Liv?"

"When she stopped by the ranch to ask directions to Drew and Sadie's house."

"Liv stopped by here?" Sam chewed on that thought. She'd walked out on him, and he hadn't seen the woman in five years. Yet, she had zero hesitation about coming around his family's cattle ranch.

The woman had gumption. He'd give her that.

She'd moved on, yet here he was, struggling to embrace a water-over-the-bridge attitude. And failing. Every single day, he got up in the house he'd built for her. The white ranch house with its wraparound porch was supposed to be a surprise wedding gift.

Yeah, moving on had proved to be a challenge.

Gramps nodded. "Miss Olivia stopped by here on the way to visit the new baby. Apparently, she's friends with your brother's wife." He shrugged. "Who knew?"

Who knew? Not him. That was certain. He'd been gone a week, and Liv was not only back but had wheedled her way into the good graces of his older brother and his sister-in-law and had managed to end up as his tenant for the next twelve months. Sam sank into a kitchen chair.

"She handed me a check," Gramps continued. "And I gave her the keys to the building. Didn't have time to deposit the check for you, but since her daddy owns the largest cattle ranch in the area, I'm guessing she's good for the money."

"You gave her the keys already?"

"She had a mighty persuasive story. Needs to get everything up and running for the Memorial Day tourist crowd. That's only four-and-a-half weeks away." His grandfather raised his palms in gesture. "Not sure how she's gonna do that without a whole lotta prayer and a few willing helpers."

Once again, Sam held his tongue because he knew she'd get it done. Liv could talk a thirsty man out of his water bottle with one smile. Yeah, the woman was dangerous.

"You're not mad at me, are you?" Gramps offered a weak smile. "It wasn't my intention to put you between a rock and a hard place."

"No, of course not." Sam worked to formulate a plan. "Do you have a number for the attorney?"

"The attorney?" Gramps closed his mouth and cleared his throat. "I do. I surely do." He hurried from the room, his boots clomping on the wooden floor, and returned with a file folder. "Everything is in here."

Sam opened the folder, and his eyes rounded at the sight of the check. That would buy a nice CNC machine for his woodshop. A high-end piece of woodworking equipment he'd put on the back burner due to the cost.

Nope. Focus, Sam.

A new machine wouldn't solve the issue at hand. Liv renting his building would remain a thunderstorm on his horizon, and he couldn't have impending disaster following his steps for the next year. He'd spent too much time trying to heal after she'd stomped on his heart. The woman had to go.

He punched in the attorney's number only to receive a recording that the office was closed until next Thursday. Today was Friday. There was no way he could wait that long.

Damage control was essential before the situation blew out of control. He stood.

"Where're you going?"

"Into town."

"Mind your temper, son."

Sam calmed at the words, a smile touching his lips. He was only seventeen when Gramps had come to live at the Lazy M after the death of Sam's parents. There was more than love between him and the elder

Morgan. There was a bond of respect. His grandfather was right. He needed to let his head rule, not his emotions. If he did, maybe he'd have a chance at convincing Liv to tear up the contract.

"Yes, sir. I will," Sam finally returned.

"Don't you want your cinnamon rolls?"

"I'll be back for them." Sam pointed a finger at his grandfather. "No taste testing while I'm gone."

"Who? Me?" Gramps chuckled. "Never."

One look at the sky on the drive into town had Sam concerned. Low-hanging cumulonimbus clouds hovered in the direction of downtown Homestead Pass, their flat tops an indication of impactful weather ahead.

He turned on the radio for a weather update. "A tornado watch has been issued for Beckham County," the radio voice droned. "A tornado watch indicates that conditions are favorable for tornados. Please be aware of severe thunderstorms in the area and stay tuned for updates."

Tornado season in Oklahoma. He was well versed in tornado response and could only pray that the watch didn't evolve into a warning indicative of tornado activity.

Despite the threat of storms and the blanket of humidity that hung in the air, downtown Homestead Pass was bustling. Sam was forced to park across the way from the building he owned on Main Street. He spotted Liv's old beater pickup truck parked at the curb of the building immediately. The cherry-red vintage Ford F-100 she'd bought in high school had more dents than not. Sam cut the ignition on his shiny black dually and got out.

For moments, he stared at the building in front of him. Part of a long row of shops, the Snodgrass Building's facade wore light brown and red brick, which framed the storefront windows. The second floor, once apartments, was now used for storage. Its expansive rectangular windows were divided into multiple tiny panes, giving the building a whimsical charm.

The front door opened on the left side of the building, catching his attention as Olivia Moretti stepped onto the sidewalk.

Sam's heart stuttered.

He'd recognize Liv in a room filled with hundreds of people. There was something about her graceful movements, no doubt credited to years of studying ballet. When she injured her ankle one too many times, she'd turned to cooking. Her dark hair was shorter than usual, and now the curls she'd called disreputable and unruly kissed her shoulders.

She took a box out of the pickup's bed and then stacked another two on top. Juggling them, she turned toward the building.

Sam strode across the street and had his hand on the doorknob before he realized what he was doing.

"Thank you," Liv said. Turning her head a fraction as she stepped over the threshold, her dark eyes widened. "Sam!"

The breathy response wrapped around Sam. He'd missed the sound of his name on her tongue.

"I wasn't expecting you."

"And I could say the same."

Flustered, her steps faltered, and the boxes swayed as if in slow motion. "I…"

Sam's hands brushed hers as he scooped the cartons from her arms and set them on the polished oak counter next to an ancient cash register. "Got 'em." He moved to the other side of the counter, far away from any further accidental contact.

"What are you doing here?" she asked.

Sam crossed his arms. Was it wrong that he took pleasure in the fact that for the first time in a very long time he held the upper hand with Liv?

He glanced around, noting that the electricity was on in the building. She certainly hadn't wasted any time. For a moment, he stared at the old schoolhouse light fixture that bathed the space in a golden warmth.

"Hello?" she prodded.

"I'm your landlord."

"No. Your grandfather signed the paperwork." Liv slowly shook her head, looking confused. "My attorney said the building belongs to Lazy M Ranch."

"He was mistaken. This is my building." Sam pinned her with his gaze. "I think we have a few things to discuss. Don't you?"

Liv opened her mouth and then closed

it again. A silence hung between them, thicker than the air outside. Finally, a resigned sigh slipped from her lips. "Okay. Sure. Why not?"

"Surprised to see you back here," Sam said.

"Surprised? Why?"

Sam silently stared at her. He'd rehearsed what he'd say to the woman who broke his heart and derailed his life. Yet now that Liv stood in front of him, all he wanted to know was why. Why, Liv? Yeah, that was the question he couldn't ask without revealing how vulnerable he remained some five years later.

"You were in such a rush to leave. I'm pretty sure there's still skid marks outside the Homestead Pass Community Church where you peeled out of the parking lot after our counseling session with the pastor."

"I sent you a letter. I apologized." She bit her lip and narrowed her eyes. In defense or concern?

His jaw tightened. "Yep. You sent me a letter." If the words sounded bitter that's because they were. Sending him a letter had been a cowardly slap in the face that continued to gall him.

"Is that why you're here?" Liv asked. "To give me a piece of your mind?"

"Not exactly."

The deep rumbling of thunder echoed in the distance, followed by a crack of lightning. Liv moved to the window and peered at the sky.

A worried expression crossed her face. "Whatever you want, can it wait?" she asked. "I've got to get the rest of the boxes out of the flatbed before it rains."

He pushed himself off the display case he'd been leaning against. "I'll help you."

Her eyes widened. "That's not necessary."

"I'll help you move the boxes," he said firmly. "Then I'd like a minute of your time to discuss the contract."

Liv exhaled sharply, then stared at him long and hard. "Why? Didn't you get my check?"

"I did." Sam refused to give her an inch. Once again, the silence stretched.

"Okay, fine," Liv said. "You want to talk. We can talk." Turning on her heel, she marched through the front door to the truck, her back straight. Clearly, not happy.

That made two of them.

Sam followed her outside. Yep, they were going to talk. He'd waited a long time for this reunion, and he had plenty to say, including half a dozen good reasons why she shouldn't rent his building.

Liv sighed.

Again.

It was all she could do. Though she came from a family of drama queens, she did not do drama. No matter how many buttons Sam Morgan pushed, she refused to argue with him.

She silently navigated around him, hauling box after box of supplies into the space that would soon be Moretti's Farm-to-Table Bistro. After years of helping other businesses launch, she would finally see her own dream become a reality.

With each step, she snuck peeks at Sam, trying to figure out what he was thinking.

It seemed unfortunate that he had only become more handsome in the years since they parted. It would have made things much easier if he'd grown a third eye or horns.

Instead, his blue eyes seemed bluer. Was that possible? Though he'd always been tall, the man appeared taller, his shoulders broader and the muscles in his forearms more pronounced. Even his dark hair seemed to have matured, going from unruly waves to well-behaved and stylishly cut.

Liv had heard from her aunt that he helped with his family's ranch and taught business classes at Oklahoma State University. He'd evolved, which surprised her because she'd pegged Sam as a lifelong professional cowboy.

Maybe she'd been wrong. After all, today, he wasn't even wearing his usual Stetson to cover his head. Sam didn't look anything like a cowboy, given his blue dress shirt and neatly creased slacks. He wasn't even wearing boots.

Still, regret filled her with each glance,

not for the choices made but for hurting him. Sam was a good man and deserved a future with a woman who could give him what he needed. She was not that woman. Unlike her mother, Liv was unwilling to give up her dreams in exchange for anyone else's. No, she could not walk the path to the future that her father and Sam had paved for her so many years ago.

But they could work together today. They did for an hour as the sky outside loomed dark and foreboding. After retrieving the last box, Liv dusted off her hands and grabbed a tote of personal items from the truck. She stared up at the sky and shivered. She'd grown up in Homestead Pass and lived through many bad-weather seasons. It never got easy.

"Is that it?" Sam asked from somewhere behind her.

"Yes. That's the last of them. Thank you." She turned on her heel and found herself face-planting into his chest. As she did, his hands grasped her forearms.

"Oh, oh. I'm sorry." She stumbled over the words, jerking back from the warmth of his arms. Strong arms she remembered all too well.

He glanced away but said nothing. Was he also disturbed by the contact?

"Yoo-hoo!" A knock at the door frame had them both turning. The smiling face of Mrs. Pickett from the bookstore across the street greeted them. "Sorry to interrupt. I saw you moving boxes and thought I better stop by. Have you been listening to the weather? Doesn't look good. Most everyone in town is closing shop and heading home." She'd continued to talk without taking a breath.

"Yes, ma'am. We're watching," Sam said.

"All right, then. Stay safe."

"We will," Liv said. "Thanks for letting us know."

Mrs. Pickett shot a curious glance between Liv and Sam. "So nice to see you two back together again."

"No, ma'am," Sam said. "We're not—"

A vehicle's horn interrupted Sam's response.

"Oh, that's my son. I better get going. He

has stops to make." Mrs. Pickett wiggled her fingers in a wave. "Toodle-loo."

"Great," Sam muttered. "Now the grapevine will be buzzing."

"You and I are old news," Liv returned.

"Easy for you to say."

She faced him, girding herself for the conversation she'd avoided for far too long.

"We're going to talk about the past now, Sam?"

"Did you see Mrs. Pickett's reaction? You're back in town like it's no big deal. But I'm the guy who will have to field all the curious and pitying glances once again. Poor Sam Morgan. Dumped by his fiancée six days before the wedding. Practically jilted at the altar."

"I'm sorry." Liv paused, searching for the right words. Were there right words? "It was never my intention to humiliate you."

"No?"

"No. What happened was about my father and me."

Back then, she was suffocating. Once she'd received her culinary arts degree, she began working in fine restaurants, training in everything from barback to sous-chef. Liv divided her time between Oklahoma and various locations, learning her craft. At twenty-nine, she was ready to move out of the nest and launch the next phase of her career, but her father had balked. He demanded that she settle down and get married and prepare to take over M&M Ranch.

Anthony Moretti had lost his wife. How could she deny him?

She couldn't. So, the obedient only child of the widowed rancher had said yes when Sam proposed. Then she panicked and did the unthinkable. Left town a week before the wedding. Yes, she was a coward—a coward who still cared for Sam. Always had, and maybe always would. However, with big dreams of a future in the culinary industry, she simply was not ready for marriage, and lacked the courage to explain how she felt to her father and Sam in person.

Her father had forgiven her. Would Sam ever be able to?

Sam's blue eyes became frigid. "I was collateral damage?"

Liv stared at him, feeling the sting of his icy glance. She couldn't blame him. It wasn't until she left that she realized how selfish she had been, failing to consider the big picture for the man who'd remained behind in Homestead Pass. A dozen times she'd nearly reached out to apologize again for her betrayal. But she hadn't, thinking the best thing she could do for Sam was to maintain her distance.

How ironic that he was now her landlord.

"I'm sorry, Sam. Truly sorry. I hope someday you can forgive me."

"You don't want to explain?"

"I explained in the letter."

"Liv, I never read your letter. Burned the thing and tossed your ring into Homestead Pass Lake."

She gasped at the harsh words.

"Maybe you can look me in the eye and tell me why you left."

Liv stared at her clasped hands for a moment as heat warmed her face. She was in the hot seat and deserved it. Could she make him understand the fear and panic that haunted her back then?

"Sam, my father had my future all lined up. Marry you, give him grandbabies, give up on my plans. I was confused."

"You ran instead of talking to the man you promised to marry? Being confused isn't a free pass for you to humiliate me in front of all of Homestead Pass."

"You're right. Again, I apologize. Far too late. But I am sorry. Very sorry that you paid the price for my poor judgment."

Once again, a rumble sounded. This time, the windows rattled. A lightning strike lit up the room, and the hanging schoolhouse lamps overhead flickered.

"Considering the weather situation, could we postpone this discussion and skip to the rental agreement?" she asked. "You had an issue with the contract?"

When he crossed his arms, Liv braced herself for a challenge.

"Yeah. You might say that. I'd like you to cancel the contract."

"What do you mean? Your grandfather approved everything. Are you going to tell me this town isn't big enough for both of us?" Though she was unable to hide her dismay, Sam's face remained an unreadable mask.

"Sam, please don't do this. There isn't another place in Homestead Pass that is adequate for my needs. This shop has a fully equipped kitchen and a walk-in freezer. It's ideal for my restaurant."

"Even if we proceed, I can only rent one side of the building."

"I was promised both sides. The contract I signed four days ago says both shops."

"What do you need the other side for?" he asked.

"A home goods boutique focusing on kitchen products." She paused. "I think the question here is, why don't you want me to have it?"

He stared at her, jaw set, blue eyes unyielding.

"It's well past seventy-two hours," she said. "I signed the contract, paid a year of rent, and I have excellent references. You don't have legal standing here."

"I have plans for the other shop," he said. "Renting it out was an error."

"Will you at least tell me what your plans are?"

"My idea is to sell handcrafted wood products." He stared her down as if in challenge.

"What does that mean? Furniture?"

"Smaller. Think signs, cutting boards, small decorative pieces."

"Oh." She paused, unsure how to proceed. "Who's your supplier?"

"I am. I'm the artist."

"You?" *Since when?* Liv stood very still, knowing her reaction could alienate him even further. That would not be helpful to her cause.

"Yes. Me," Sam returned.

"I had no idea you were a craftsman."

"Yeah. I know. You think I'm another Oklahoma cowboy whose life begins on the ranch."

He pointedly assessed her Wranglers and red cowboy boots, the irony unspoken.

Uh-oh. Now she'd done it. Instead of soothing the beast, she'd poked the bear.

"I never said that. I'm just surprised."

"Why surprised? I've always messed around with my father's tools." He shrugged, looked at her and then away. Clearly, he wasn't going to elaborate.

Messed around. Yes, exactly. In the past, Sam often retreated to his father's workshop when he needed to think. She had no idea it would become a career path.

Liv paced back and forth across the room, thinking. They wanted the same thing. Fulfilling her plans depended on coming up with a solution. A reasonable compromise would be good.

She blinked as an idea popped into her head. "Consignment."

"What?" he asked.

"I said consignment." She turned to him. "I'd be happy to consign your wood products in my shop."

"*My* shop," he returned.

"Now you're being unreasonable." She frowned. "I think you're reneging on the agreement because you simply don't want to rent to me. This is personal."

Another rumble of thunder interrupted

the conversation, this time much closer. They both turned to the windows as pelting rain tap-danced against the glass.

Sam pulled out his phone. "Weather app shows several storms on the radar. This one is right over Homestead Pass." He glanced at the ceiling. "Guess we'll find out if the roof leaks or not."

"Why did you buy this building?" she asked. It seemed an odd venture for a man who owned one-fourth of a cattle ranch.

"Couldn't pass up the deal that T.D. Snodgrass offered."

"I don't believe I've ever met a Snodgrass in Homestead Pass, though I recall the various shops in this spot over the years."

"There hasn't been a Snodgrass in town in over sixty years," Sam said. "T.D. inherited it from his father. He lives in Elk City but continued to rent the place out for years. When T.D. retired and sold all his properties, he gave me the building for five dollars. It includes the parking lot next door, that I share with the inn."

"Wow, that was generous of him." She

shook her head. "But why would he give you a building for five bucks?"

"He was my first customer when I passed my accounting certification."

"You're a CPA?" Liv was utterly confused. Sam Morgan, the guy she'd watched ride broncs at the local rodeos, was a certified public accountant.

"After you left, I went back to college to get my master's degree in business and then took the exam on a whim. I never charged T.D. because he was my test client."

"A CPA." Liv worked to process his admission. He'd been very busy since she'd been gone—and not riding bucking broncs. She blinked realizing what his words meant for her. "I guess now that you're the lord of the land, you've decided I'm persona non grata."

"Nope. That's not it at all."

A drop of water plopped on Liv's arm, and she stared at the moisture. "Oh no."

Both she and Sam looked up at the ceiling.

Sam gestured out the window where

rapid streams of water rushed down Main Street. "Flash flooding. We'll have to stay put until it eases."

She glanced around. "Maybe we should slide the boxes farther away from the windows."

"I left a few tarps in the supply room after I painted the place. I'll grab them."

Liv checked her phone for messages when he disappeared behind a door down the hall.

A few minutes later, he returned with two blue tarps under one arm and a bucket in his hand. He placed the bucket beneath the leak and dropped the tarps on the floor.

"Where do we stack the boxes?" she asked.

"The hallway. May as well prepare for a worst-case scenario." He looked at the cardboard storage cartons and plastic containers. "How many of these are for the other shop?"

"None of them."

He turned his eyes on her. Surprise flickered in the blue depths. "This is all for this side?"

"Yes. This is my first load." Now she regretted not starting earlier. She'd vowed to spend more time with her father and had lingered at the ranch all morning.

The lights flickered, and the wind howled, reminding them to hurry.

"If the sirens go off, we're going to have to take cover," Sam said. He reached for a box and pushed it into the hall.

Over and over again, they slid or carried boxes in silent haste. It only took twenty minutes until they filled the hall with stacks of them, leaving a narrow path to the back of the shop. Together they spread the tarp and tucked the edges under the boxes.

"That should do it," Sam said.

"Thank you," Liv said. "Considering how you feel about your new tenant, that was very generous of you."

"I'm not the bad guy, Liv."

"Maybe you should consider that I'm not either," she said softly.

He strode to the window and searched the sky. "The rain has stopped for now.

We both should head home before the next storm passes through."

"You don't want to settle our difference of opinion today?" she asked.

"It is settled. I want the other shop."

"Sam."

"I'll be by early tomorrow to look at the roof. We can talk more then."

More talking. The Sam Morgan she used to know wasn't a talker. He'd certainly changed. But what choice did she have?

He pulled his key fob from his pocket. "You're going back to M&M, right?"

"Yes. My father and my aunt will be waiting. I'm going to make a couple of phone calls first."

Calls to verify the shipping dates for the display units she'd ordered. They'd be the centerpiece of the home goods boutique she'd be opening next door. But he didn't need to know that.

Sam nodded and turned away without sparing her another glance.

His silence cut, though there was no

doubt she deserved his scorn. Somehow, she'd make it up to him and convince him they could work together. Somehow.

Chapter Two

~❧~

Sam got in his truck and started the engine. For minutes, he sat there, disgusted with himself. What had he done? Left things unresolved when he meant to put an end to the situation. His brothers would never let him live this down if they found out.

They'd labeled big brother Drew the optimist. His younger brothers were fraternal twins. Trevor, the cynic, and Lucas, the jokester.

Sam was the pushover. Well, no more. Those days were officially over.

A quick perusal of the sky through the rain-dotted windshield of his pickup truck told him that though the rain had stopped, another wall of threatening clouds had moved in.

The almost hazy green tint brought back memories of his father. *Look for the green clouds, son. That means the wind has sucked up the frogs and a tornado is on the way.*

He would have thought that, by now, he'd have his own kids to share that fable with. Sam rolled down his window and inhaled the pungent zing of vegetation and ozone in the unusually calm air.

A chill inched up his arms. Everything within him screamed that a tornado was in the vicinity.

Hail began to ping off his windshield, like marbles, and the inevitable warning sirens blasted into the air. That meant a tornado was imminent.

Sam closed the window and punched in his brother Drew's number on his cell phone. The eldest Morgan sibling answered immediately.

"Where are you?" Drew asked. "We have sirens going off out here."

"I'm in town. Everyone accounted for at the ranch?"

"Yeah, I'm not concerned about the ranch. Weather report says a twister was spotted north of town. Headed directly for you."

"I'll take cover. A few prayers would be appreciated."

"You got it, Sam. Stay safe, and give me a call when it's over."

"Will do."

He pushed open the truck door with his shoulder against the force of the gusting winds. The streets of Homestead Pass were empty as he dodged blowing branches and debris to get across the street.

When he entered the building, he found Liv at the window, staring at the sky.

"Get away from there," he growled. "You know better."

"You're right." She wrapped her arms around herself and moved backward until she was against the store counter. Shaking her head as if waking up, she grabbed her tote bag from the floor.

"Liv, we need to get into the restroom area. It's the center of the building."

Anguish filled her eyes. "I have to grab my recipes. They're my mother's."

"There's no time."

Her gaze went to the hallway. "I know which box they're in."

Sam relented against his better judgment. He understood the pain of a lost parent and the importance of treasured mementos. Following Liv as she raced down the hall and removed the tarp from the first stack of boxes, he offered up a silent prayer for protection.

A powerful lightning arc crackled outside, and a moment later, the lights went out, plunging the shop into darkness. Though it was only noon, it seemed like midnight. Sam's heart thudded as the whistling wind hammered the building.

He put a hand on Liv's arm. "We have to take cover. Now."

Behind them, a crash reverberated into the shop, along with the sound of shattering glass.

Liv screamed as the front window imploded. Glass and tree debris shot into the store. Branches and leaves flew across the room.

Sam quickly snaked his arm around Liv's waist, his other hand reaching for the tarp as he pulled her into the restroom and slammed the door shut.

"Get down," he commanded, pulling the material over them.

"Wh-wh-what was that?" Liv asked.

"My guess is a tree sailed through the storefront."

"A tree." She repeated the words through trembling lips.

"It's going to be okay." Head bowed, he pulled her close and put an arm around her shoulders beneath the protection of the tarp. "Hey, at least it wasn't a cow," he murmured.

"What do we do now?" she asked. "At home, we get in the bathtub and put a mattress over ourselves."

"Yeah, note to self. Get a tub in here."

He could barely see Liv in the darkness. She stared at him with eyes round with fear. "I know you're joking to keep me calm. But don't think I don't appreciate that you probably saved my life."

"Oh, I think the Big Guy upstairs had a hand in keeping us safe. But it's not over yet, so keep praying."

Outside, the wind continued to roar. The small glass-block window of the restroom rattled as the wind pushed against the blocks, insistent in its demand to enter.

"Duck down," Sam yelled over the increasing din.

The glass rattled a few more times before it suddenly stopped.

For long minutes, they sat listening.

Sam shoved the tarp out of the way and pulled out his phone. Ten minutes had passed since he'd called his brother. It seemed a lifetime ago.

"It's so quiet," Liv said, her breath warm against his cheek. "Do you think it's safe to go out there?"

"I don't know."

His phone began to ding repeatedly. Then it started ringing. Sam glanced at the screen. It was Drew.

"Yeah, I'm all right," he told his brother.

"Could you call the M&M Ranch and let them know Liv is safe?" He glanced at Liv as his brother tossed out questions that he couldn't answer right now with Liv listening. "I'll explain later," Sam said. "I've got to assess the damage here, and then I'll head home."

He helped Liv to her feet, and they staggered through the doorway into the hall.

"My boxes," Liv wailed.

Sam turned to see a mountain of boxes shoved into a heap, some misshapen, where they'd been slammed against the back wall. Others were wet from the tornado's path through the building.

"You're alive. Let's thank God for that. My mother used to say that people are more important than things."

She gave a resigned sigh. "Yes, of course. I'll try to remember that as I go through those boxes."

Together, they kicked debris and glass that littered the floor out of the way while making their way to the front of the shop.

"It is a tree," Liv said. "Right in the middle of the window."

The clouds had lifted outside, and blue skies illuminated the space, revealing that, indeed, a huge redbud had been uprooted from the sidewalk and now sat halfway inside the shop, its massive trunk spanning the sidewalk. The other end of the tree rested on Liv's truck.

"My truck!"

"We'll call for a tow," he said.

Sam peered around the tree, across the street at his own truck. Though leaves and sticks littered the hood and cab, there didn't appear to be any damage.

"I can't believe that truck made it through my teenage escapades only to be hit by a tornado," Liv said.

"All cosmetic. It will be back on the road in no time."

A quick glance at Liv said she wasn't comforted. His attention moved to her upper arm, where a bright red stain had seeped through her pink T-shirt. *Blood.*

"Liv, you're bleeding." Alarmed, he moved to her side.

"What?" She looked down at her arm.

"It's a cut from the flying glass. It's not deep."

"Yeah, but it's still bleeding." Sam pulled out a pocketknife.

"What are you doing?"

"Making a pressure pad." He cut a sleeve from his dress shirt, tore off the button and folded the material into a square. "Hold this against the cut."

She complied. "I'm fine."

"Right. Sure." Sam nodded, doing his best to pretend he was unaffected by the sight of her skin marred by the laceration.

"Let's go outside," he said. "But watch where you step."

"The door is gone," Liv said.

"Yeah, I noticed." He stepped over the threshold onto the sidewalk, where the traffic light hung askew at the corner of Main Street and Edison Avenue. Tree branches, leaves, and a few overturned vehicles littered the streets. The sight seemed postapocalyptic.

Sam stepped onto the street to assess the building's exterior. A dozen or so bricks lay on the sidewalk, but the edifice seemed otherwise intact. He'd have it checked out by an engineer to be sure it remained structurally sound.

Next door in the other shop, windows had shattered as well. The space held overturned display shelves in a tangled mess against a wall. Glass and debris covered every inch of the floor.

Liv groaned as she joined him. "What a mess." The words were as bleak as the expression on her face.

"Yeah, this is going to take some time."

Behind them, a soft tap of a vehicle horn sounded. They turned to see a Homestead Pass Police Department vehicle moving slowly down Main Street toward them. The black-and-white SUV stopped at the curb. The familiar face of Steve Keller, Homestead Pass's local police deputy, greeted them.

"You two okay?" His gaze took in the blood on Liv's arm. "I can call a medic to check your arm."

"Good idea," Sam said.

"I'm fine," Liv returned.

When Sam opened his mouth to contradict her, Liv glared at him.

"It's a scratch." She removed the pad. "See. It's already stopped bleeding."

Steve grinned. "So, you two are back together again, huh? About time."

"No!" Liv and Sam denied the observation in unison.

"Okay, okay." Steve held up a palm. "If you're all right, I'm going to keep going, then. I have a lot of ground to cover. Literally."

Sam nodded. "Hey, Steve. Was the hardware store hit?"

"No. The funnel only hit this side of the street and jumped over to the next block. Rope tornado. Dissipated now." He assessed the Snodgrass Building. "Looks to me like your building sustained the greatest impact. Though I talked to the folks next door at the inn, and they lost windows and tell me they have roof damage."

Sam nodded, relieved to hear the situation wasn't as bad as he'd feared.

The deputy nodded and drove farther down the street.

"Hardware store?" Liv asked.

"We'll need to board things up for tonight."

"What about that tree?" she asked.

He assessed the tree from all angles. "Chainsaw."

"Then what?" Liv looked at him with hope in her eyes.

Sam glanced away. He would not be caught in the gaze of those big brown eyes. "Then, I'm your landlord. I'll see to it that repairs are done in a timely manner."

"How timely?"

He shot her a sharp look. They were thirty minutes post-tornado. Was she seriously going to pressure him about repairs before he'd even done a complete evaluation of the damage? Unbelievable.

"Look, I appreciate that we are fortunate to be unscathed after a run-in with a tornado..."

"But what?" Sam tensed, waiting for her response.

"I'd like to be ready to open, even with a small menu, by Memorial Day."

He glared, unable to believe what he had

just heard. "Are you kidding me? This is the first week of May."

"Sam, you know how important Memorial Day is. If I can get a tourist buzz going, the business has a prayer of making it through to Labor Day. Summer is peak income-earning time for businesses in small towns like Homestead Pass." She frowned. "Everything slows down come September."

"Don't you have to hire staff and get equipment in?"

"All of that is in progress. You forget, I do this for a living."

"No. I don't know what you do for a living these days. The only thing I know is that before your hasty departure, I only saw you a few times a month, if that." She'd been commuting back and forth from Homestead Pass to different jobs all over Oklahoma.

"It's not like you were around much either," she returned. "If you weren't working at the Lazy M, you were on the rodeo circuit most weekends."

"Yeah, but I'm not the one who walked

out." The words came out harsher than intended. He was surprised at the flash of something close to anger that surged through him. Hadn't he buried those emotions?

"There's no need to get testy," Liv returned. "I thought, maybe, after sitting through a tornado together, you might be less resistant to the idea of me renting your property." She paused. "I'm here to stay, Sam. Eventually you're going to have to make peace with that."

He stared at her wordlessly. They'd been through more than a tornado together. He'd known this woman for what seemed like a lifetime and the relationship had meant everything to him. She was a freshman in high school, and he was a senior when they met. Once upon a time he saw his future in Olivia Moretti.

Now, the only thing he saw was betrayal.

He dug in his pocket for keys. "Maybe you should give your family an update while I'm gone."

"I'll do that. And maybe you can think about what I said."

Sam crossed the street to his truck, shaking his head. There was nothing to think about beyond patching up his building for the night. There was no way he'd let his guard down enough to allow Liv to become his world again.

Liv yawned and reached for another box. She opened the flaps of the wet cardboard and groaned. Sunset had settled on Homestead Pass, hampering her ability to check the contents of the boxes for damage. What she needed was a flashlight and maybe a chocolate bar. She'd eaten a bag of chips and a hot dog from the food truck at the hardware store, but that was hours ago.

"I'm heading out. Do you want a ride home?" Sam stood over her, frowning.

It seemed all he did was frown. They'd worked together for hours, yet he'd hardly spoken a word.

"Yes. Thank you." Liv unfolded her legs and got to her feet. "Are you done?" she asked.

"I've got the plywood on the windows and doors. *Done* is a goal for another day."

Liv picked up her tote bag and followed him outside. He put the chain and padlock on the front door and joined her on the sidewalk, where she stared at her pitiful truck.

Sam had removed the tree with the help of Deputy Keller, but what remained was a flattened version of the pickup. It was almost comical. She wouldn't be surprised if two clowns popped out of the front seat. That's what kind of day today had been.

"Did you call for a tow?" Sam asked.

"Yes. I'm on the list."

"That's something." He pointed to his truck across the street. "Keep an eye out for traffic. That streetlight is still out."

The silence continued as they climbed into the dually, and he guided the vehicle down Main Street, out of town.

Once they reached the town limits, Sam cleared his throat, and she sensed his discomfort at the silence. "How's your arm?" he asked.

She touched the edges of the bandage. "It's fine, but I'm pretty sure calling that paramedic over to check on me was unnecessary."

"Look how you jump to conclusions, assuming it was me. Steve probably did it."

"You're a terrible fibber."

Sam kept his eyes on the road, revealing nothing. "Think positive. Now your tetanus vaccine is up to date."

"I'll let Steve know," she returned.

"I hear you met Andrew Scott Morgan Jr.," he said.

"Your nephew. Yes, I did." She grinned. "You're Uncle Sam now."

"Yeah, that's the standing joke at the ranch. I'm glad I can entertain everyone."

Liv chuckled. "I think it's cute."

"Yeah, real cute."

Liv smiled, recalling her visit with Drew and Sadie Morgan. They were so happy. A baby boy and a toddler rounded out their family. Liv knew that a small part of her envied what Drew and Sadie had. She hadn't ruled out a family of her own, but she'd know if and when the time was right.

"The baby is two weeks old?" she asked.

"Correct. I was afraid I'd miss the excitement, but little Andy was kind enough to arrive right before I left for Vegas."

"Vegas? You're a gambler now?"

"Not hardly. I subscribe to the theory that the best way to double your money is to fold it and put it in your pocket. I went to an ag and ranching conference in Drew's place."

She nodded slowly. "And are you still rodeoing?"

Sam laughed. "I'm thirty-eight this year. Way too old for that nonsense."

Way too old? There was nothing old about Sam. He was a handsome man, and she felt certain that the women of Homestead Pass had him listed on their eligible bachelor list.

"You're still working on the Lazy M?"

He glanced at her. "You sure have a lot of questions."

The rest of the sentence hung between them. *A lot of questions for a woman who walked away from me.*

Liv found herself annoyed and defensive, and she didn't like the feeling. "I'm just making conversation."

"For the record, I am employed by Lazy M Ranch as an accountant. I've spent a lifetime in the dust. Ranching and rodeo are a young man's job. I'm strictly a desk wrangler now unless Trevor is short-handed."

She couldn't believe what she was hearing. "You used to love the rodeo and the ranch."

"Rodeo is an Oklahoma rite of passage. As for the ranch, cattle have never been my first love." He shrugged. "Don't get me wrong. I love the Lazy M and know I'm blessed to be part of the operation. But it's not my whole life. The ranch doesn't define me."

Liv mulled his response, surprised to realize they had more in common than ever. That thought gave her pause.

The ranch doesn't define me, he'd said. She hadn't given Sam enough credit. He'd broken free of the box she put him in.

Well, she could say the same; M&M Ranch did not define her. She was the daughter of a rancher who was dead-set determined she'd continue his legacy. Maybe once her businesses were up and running, her father would get it and be proud of what she'd accomplished.

That thought brought her back to today's events. How would she get her timeline back on schedule?

"About the shops…" she began.

"What about the shops?" Sam stretched his neck back and forth as he drove.

"When will repairs start?"

"Tomorrow."

"Oh, that's great. I'll be there with boxes for the other side."

He frowned but said nothing, his hands gripping the steering wheel and his attention on the road.

"Is that a problem?" she asked.

"Not a problem."

"Not a problem because I have a signed contract or because you're still going to try to kick me out?"

"Tell me again what your business is about," Sam said, sidestepping the question.

"Kitchen and dining goods. Distinctive home accessories."

"And you think there's a big market for that in Homestead Pass?" Sam shook his head. "Did you know that Bess Lowder has used the same cast-iron skillet for thirty years?"

"As long as people like to cook, there will be a market for the products my shop will offer. Besides, it's not just pots and pans. I've got a vendor with an entire line of imported olive oil. Oh, and teas and coffee. And another bringing in adorable, small table lamps. Things that normally have to be ordered online or can only be found in Oklahoma City or Tulsa in specialty shops."

"Adorable lamps?" Sam grimaced. "How can you afford to stock that kind of stuff and still turn a profit?" He raised a hand from the steering wheel and offered her a palm. "Don't answer that. I forget that you're a Moretti."

Liv gasped. "I can't believe you said that. It's not like I'm a trust fund baby. You know better."

"Okay. Okay. I'm sorry. I might be a little cranky. I don't sleep well in hotels."

"Apology accepted. For your information, I've invested my entire savings into this venture. My father wholly disapproves and sees my career choice as another interference in his plans for my future."

"That's kinda harsh."

"Is it?" Liv sucked in a breath and silently shook her head. Through no fault of his own, Sam failed to appreciate the pressure she'd been under all her life to continue her father's vision for the future.

Liv had been raised with a silent code of loyalty that demanded that family business stayed in the family. She rarely spoke about her father's misguided plans. Not even to Sam.

Years later and not a thing had changed. Her father continued to insist that she get married and have a dozen kids so her husband and children could inherit the ranch. Liv's mother had been the only one who could make him see reason.

"I'm sure Anthony is proud of you," Sam said.

Liv scoffed louder than she intended at the words.

"My father has a long list of requirements before I get the daughter-of-the-year award."

"Why don't you talk to him?" Sam guided the truck around a downed branch in the road as he spoke.

"All this time, and nothing has changed."

"What about his sister?" Sam asked. "Isn't Chef Moretti still teaching classes at the Homestead Pass Inn?"

"Aunt Loretta? Yes. And she does catering on the side." Liv paused. "She's the one who gave me the idea to open the restaurant here. But she has zero leverage with my father. He considers her a bad influence because she never married."

"Since your aunt's a chef like you, will she help you launch the restaurant?"

"She's made it clear that if I need her, she's available. Aunt Loretta understands the danger of too many cooks in the kitchen." Liv smiled. "Eventually, she'll move her cooking classes from the inn to my restaurant. She can run classes when the restaurant is closed."

Sam nodded. "Mind if I ask why you

decided to move back? You could have opened a restaurant anywhere."

Anywhere but his town. The unspoken words hung between them. He was right and it seemed an irony that she would return to Homestead Pass.

Liv stared out the window at the cloudless sky.

"Is that a hard question?" Sam tapped his fingers on the steering wheel, then looked at her.

"Yes, I guess it is." Liv closed her eyes for a moment, reliving the moment her aunt called to let her know that her father was in the ER. "I moved back to be close to my father. He has some cardiac issues. The procedure he needs is risky due to his other health problems." She swallowed. "I'm hoping I can encourage him to slow down and delegate. He has a terrific staff at the ranch, but he's a micromanager."

Sam nodded. "I admire your dedication to your father, but asking a bull to tap dance probably isn't going to happen."

"Tell me about it."

Silence stretched for minutes. Then Sam

turned to her. "You're a good daughter, Liv," he said softly.

The kind words surprised Liv and touched her, though all the while, guilt continued to point a finger in her direction. If she were a good daughter, she wouldn't have stayed away so long.

The wrought iron, arching gates of M&M Ranch came into view. Sam stopped the truck at the code box and rolled down his window.

"It's the same code. Never changes," Liv said.

Sam said nothing, but he was probably thinking the same thing she was. Remembering how many nights he'd driven through this gate to take her home. She pushed the thought away. That was the past.

The gates slowly parted, allowing them access to the private entrance to the cattle ranch her father had built from the ground up. Sam drove down the paved road toward the family home, a grand Tudor-style house with a pitched roof and gables. The house was entirely out of place on a ranch in Oklahoma.

Yet, every time she saw the house, she was reminded of the story her father told her at bedtime about the struggling rancher and the pretty ballerina.

Anthony Moretti had met the love of his life in college. She was a British student studying in the States. They fell in love, but the girl's father disapproved of the match. It was ten more years before they were reunited. Her mother gave up her career and moved to Oklahoma. The house was a wedding present to remind her mother of home.

"I've always liked your house," Sam said.

"I like your house better. The Morgan house has that beautiful front porch I'm jealous of. I've always said that I want a white house with a big wraparound porch."

"Yep, I remember." His gaze hardened. "I don't live at the ranch house. I have a place on the spread."

"Oh." Had she said something out of line? Liv didn't know what else to say.

Things had changed between them. Had she expected everything to stay the same?

She turned in her seat. "What time will you be at the shop tomorrow?"

"Soon as the sun is up. I'll bring a generator and hook up lights until the electricity is restored."

"I'll be there." She smiled. "Thank you again, Sam."

"Don't thank me. I'm just the landlord."

Right. Just the landlord.

As she unbuckled her seat belt, the front door of the house opened, and her father stepped outside. Liv nearly groaned aloud. Anthony Moretti put a brown felt Stetson on his head and grinned, looking perkier than he had in days.

Yes, of course he was thrilled to see Sam. Sam Morgan, the son he never had, was the answer to all his prayers.

The vehicle barely rolled to a stop before Liv pushed open her door and jumped down, hoping she could hurry things along before her father said something she would regret. Ever the gentleman, Sam got out of the truck and shook her father's hand.

"Long time no see," her father said to Sam.

"Good to see you, sir."

The Moretti patriarch assessed Sam's torn shirt and Liv's bandaged arm. "You two have had quite a day." He patted Sam on the back. "Thank you for taking care of my little girl."

"Oh, I can honestly say that Olivia held her own, sir."

"Sounds like my daughter."

"Papà, I'm right here," Liv mumbled. Right here, yet her father's gaze never left Sam.

"Won't you stay for dinner, son?"

No. No. No. Liv silently pleaded.

"Thank you for the offer, sir, but in truth, I'm ready to find my pillow. I was on a plane early this morning."

"Another time, then."

"Yes, sir." Sam looked at Liv and offered a brief nod. "See you tomorrow."

He got in the dually and drove off. With the truck in the distance, her father put an arm around her shoulder. "You two have plans tomorrow? That's what I like to hear."

"Don't get too excited, Papà. It turns out that Sam is my landlord. We're working on my shops. There was damage from the storm."

"It's all good. Working together is a fine foundation for the future."

"Papà, I told you. Sam is not my future."

"We'll see." Her father grinned, his brown eyes sparkling as he turned to the house.

She shook her head at the comment. As usual, he didn't hear a word she said.

Liv followed him, noting his ever-present wheeze and his slow pace, favoring his left leg. He'd aged quickly in the last few months.

She was on her way to seeing her goals actually become reality, and she prayed her father would be around to share them with her.

Chapter Three

Liv got out of her father's truck and leaned against the door. Overhead, the last wisps of sunrise stretched across the sky, revealing no trace of yesterday's storm. A slight breeze relieved the humidity, bringing with it the scent of cinnamon, the sound of hammers and the hum of nail guns.

Her gaze spanned the busy scene before her, where people moved in and out of the Snodgrass Building. Something caught her eye, and she looked up. Two men were on the flat-top roof, tossing things down a chute and into two large commercial dumpsters that stood where her truck used to be. And in the middle of the intersection of Main Street and Edison Avenue, a worker stood in a cherry picker, diligently repairing the downed traffic light. What a difference a few hours made.

"Hey, Liv. Good to see you," Drew Morgan said. He saluted her with a lidded coffee cup as he strode past with a tool belt around his waist.

"You, too," Liv answered, somewhat perplexed to see the eldest Morgan brother here. Though all the Morgans were tall and handsome, there was no confusing them. Drew was taller than Sam, and leaner, and his hair was lighter.

"Morning." Sam joined her in the street. Today he had donned an obnoxiously loud, orange Oklahoma State University T-shirt with Wranglers and work boots. A backward navy baseball cap covered the dark hair, making him look like a kid.

She stared at him with a healthy amount of suspicion. After uttering only one word, he already seemed more agreeable than yesterday. Was this a new tactic to convince her to relinquish the shop to him?

"You, okay?" He peered at her with concern.

Liv offered a cordial greeting. "I'm fine. Why do you ask?"

"You've got a big question mark on your face."

"More like a dozen questions. Let's start with my truck."

"Towed this morning."

"Without the keys?"

"Don't need the keys to tow, but you should swing by there and drop them off and touch base with your insurance company."

"Yes. Yes. Of course." She assessed him again. "You're on top of things. It's only seven a.m. I haven't even had my second cup of coffee."

"The sun rose thirty minutes ago." He cocked his head toward the building. "And if I'm going to make any headway on cleanup, I have to use the daylight to my advantage until the electricity is restored."

"Where did all these men come from?"

"I pulled my brothers and a few wranglers away from the Lazy M."

"Who's watching the ranch?" She nearly laughed at the image of cattle sitting around, playing a rousing game of rummy while the boss was away.

"Gus is."

"You left your eighty-one-year-old grandfather in charge?"

"Gramps has more get-up-and-go than men half his age. Besides, what's the worst that can happen?"

"I'm not going to answer that." She looked at him. "So, all of your brothers are here on a Saturday?"

"Yeah, we're a team. That's how family works."

Was it? Liv processed the information. As an only child, she had zero insight into the dynamics of a family with four siblings and had often envied Sam.

She waved a hand around, encouraged by his words. "They're going to fix everything?"

"Not hardly." Sam chuckled. "There's a fair extent of damage. Fortunately, insurance will cover much of the cost. If the ranch crew can complete cleanup today, I can start on major repairs."

"Which major repairs?" She surveyed the scene before her, eager for good news. News that she could get her own projects back on track.

"The roof, for one. Though obviously, the doors and windows are top priority, followed by the walls. The floors will have to be repaired and refinished. The list goes on and on."

Liv nodded. "How can I help?"

"The good news is that your kitchen is undamaged, except for two windows, which are now boarded up. The supply rooms at the back of the shops sustained only minor water damage. If you can move your boxes there and use that area to sort, you'll...ah." He rubbed his chin as though searching for the right words.

"What? Just say it."

"Stay out of the way."

Annoyed, she straightened from her position, leaning on the truck. "I'd like nothing more than to stay out of your way."

"Don't get all defensive. You asked, and

I'm telling you. There's a liability issue here. You're my tenant."

"Okay, fine. I get it, Sam."

"Great, and maybe you should give me your phone number. In case of a landlord/tenant issue."

"I thought it was on the contract."

"No, only your attorney's information was on the paperwork."

Liv dug in her tote bag and handed him her phone. "Fine. Text your phone. Then I'll have your number as well."

The wind picked up, tossing the leaves that littered the street and bringing with it a waft of butter and cinnamon. Liv inhaled, and her stomach growled. "Do you smell cinnamon?"

"Bess dropped off enough cinnamon rolls for an army." He handed her back the cell phone and pointed to the right of the Snodgrass Building.

Cinnamon rolls? Why hadn't she thought of that? She could have whipped something up last night and would have, except that by the time she went to bed, she was physically and emotionally exhausted from yesterday's events.

"There's a table over there by the generator," Sam continued. "Hot coffee is available too."

"Thank you. Now, if you'll excuse me. This is me, getting out of your way." Liv turned on her heel and walked directly to the food table.

As she stood on the sidewalk, devouring a cinnamon roll and coffee, Trevor and Lucas Morgan appeared.

Trevor pushed back the brim of his cowboy hat and offered a nod. "Morning, Olivia."

"Um, good morning." She eyed the brothers, whom she hadn't seen since she left town. Though they were her age, from her first day of high school, she'd only had eyes for the second Morgan boy.

Lucas elbowed Trevor. "What my loquacious brother should have said is that you look as lovely as ever, Miss Moretti. Welcome back to Homestead Pass." He removed his straw Stetson and offered a bow.

"Loquacious? Now, there's a five-dollar word," Liv said with a smile.

"It was in the morning paper. The word of the day. *Loquacious.* Tending to talk a great deal. Talkative."

She laughed again. Lucas hadn't changed. He was still the charmer of the family.

"Mind if I ask your intentions?" Trevor asked.

"My intentions?" She frowned. "I intend to open a restaurant."

Lucas shook his head. "He means your intentions regarding Sam."

"Oh?" She searched both faces and realized they were very serious. A moment later, the light bulb came on, and her heart began to hammer at the unspoken accusation. "I have no intentions. Zero. Your brother is my landlord, and I'm the tenant. We have a contract. That's it."

"Glad to hear that," Trevor said, "because things were tough for Sam when you left."

"Sam was hurting," Lucas added. Concern filled the cowboy's eyes.

"I... I understand," Liv said. She was taken aback by the subtle warning from the brothers while, at the same time, touched by their fierce devotion to Sam. Had they painted her as the villain all this time? Liv blinked, distressed by the thought. Maybe she was the villain.

She waved a hand in the other direction, eager to leave the conversation. "I better get going. There are boxes to unload."

"Yes, ma'am," Lucas said with a smile and a tip of his Stetson.

Unloading boxes went faster this time since she'd remembered to bring a hand truck. Plus, she was fueled with annoyance as she replayed her conversation with the Morgan boys over and over in her head each time she rolled a stack of cartons into the store.

She'd done an awful thing, walking away from her problems. Guilt stalked her every day, but she couldn't fix the past. At the time, it seemed her only option.

Once Liv finished with the boxes, she moved to what would be her retail store. The oak floor of the shop had been swept clean and the broken shelving removed. Liv was able to quickly unload the home goods merchandise into the supply room in the back.

Things were starting to look up. Even her trip to the Homestead Pass auto shop an hour later proved productive. The insurance company would have an adjuster out on Monday, and parts were ordered for her pathetic truck.

When she returned to the Snodgrass Building, she couldn't help but notice Sam standing on the sidewalk across the street in an animated conversation with a bubbly blonde. The woman laughed and frequently touched Sam's arm in gesture.

Liv frowned and glanced away. Of course, beautiful women had always flocked to Sam. Besides being handsome, he was genuinely nice.

Then, why did the sight irritate her?

"Mindy Ellwood."

Liv turned to see Drew standing right behind her. "Pardon me?"

"Mindy Ellwood. Runs that little boutique across the street, next to the bookstore."

"I never noticed a boutique before." She glanced back at the storefronts. Glitz & Glam. Interesting name.

"Opened about a week ago. I know this because my wife told me. And she knows because Bess told her that all the women in town are up in arms because Mindy is dating all the eligible men."

"At the same time?" Liv raised a brow.

Drew laughed. "I don't know. I was changing a diaper during the conversation and wasn't paying close attention."

"Sam is very much an eligible man, so I say more power to Miss Mindy." Liv pasted on a smile for Drew.

Sam's choice of companions was his business. Not hers. She just hadn't expected to find herself so off-kilter to see him with another woman. Clearly, that was her problem, and she had better get over herself immediately because there was no time in her schedule for thinking about what could have been.

"The thing is," Drew continued, "Sam

always manages to talk himself out of relationships. I figure he's not over you yet."

"What? That's not true," Liv said, appalled at the words. Were all the Morgan men so blatantly honest? Of course Sam was over her. He'd made that point very clear.

"No?" Drew frowned. His expression said he believed otherwise.

Liv met his gaze. "Your brothers warned me away from Sam a few minutes ago."

"Trev and Luc?" He shook his head. "That's because when Sam is unhappy, he makes their lives miserable."

"It appears you're contradicting their instructions."

"Nah, I'm only sharing information." He chuckled. "Thought you might be interested."

"I'm his tenant. That's all. I have a busy and fulfilling life. Besides, Sam and I have nothing in common anymore." As she said the words, she recalled her last few conversations with Sam. The two of them just might have more in common now than in the past. Could that be true?

"Nothing in common. I think those were my exact words when I met Sadie." A phone tune rang out, and Drew pulled a cell from his pocket, and his face lit up. "Speaking of my lovely wife." He grinned like the happiest man in the world. "I'll catch you later, Liv."

Liv shot one more glance at the couple across the street. Then she pulled a stack of folded moving boxes and a roll of packing tape from the pickup and quickly moved into what would soon be her restaurant.

At the sight of the damaged boxes, she dropped the supplies in her hand in renewed dismay. Many were soggy with moisture. Others had completely fallen apart, the contents a jumble.

Though the floor had been cleaned, Liv put a piece of cardboard down to be sure there were no random slivers of glass. Then she sank to the ground, crossing her legs, and looked around, working hard to remain positive.

The space she was in would be an additional prep area and double as a room for her aunt to teach classes. She closed her eyes and opened them slowly, envisioning her restaurant. Earthy tones, raw wood, exposed brick and metal. The small courtyard behind the restaurant would be transformed to create a modest outdoor dining experience.

Overhead, the lights blinked and finally came on, illuminating the space. Outside, a hearty round of cheers echoed from Sam's crew.

A crew who worked enthusiastically under Sam's direction. She wasn't fooling herself. They were Team Sam.

Admittedly, the conversation with the Morgan boys had left her a bit off balance. She was naïve not to have considered the possibility that there were others, like Trevor and Lucas, who might be concerned that her return to Homestead Pass would hurt Sam.

Unnerved, Liv stopped what she was doing.

Then she shook it off.

She would simply have to prove herself and change their minds.

Homestead Pass was her home too, and

self-pity was a waste of time. The clock was ticking, and she had a business to build.

"I've reconsidered," Liv said.

Sam ignored the voice below his perch on the ladder.

Staying out of his way had lasted one day. It was now five in the afternoon on Sunday, and he was tired. He'd worked into the night on Saturday. After church, he'd returned and focused on the interior building repairs.

Now here she was, talking to him while he measured the windows in the restaurant for glass, seemingly unfazed by his lack of response.

"Could you hand me that pencil?" he asked.

"Pencil?" Liv looked around. "What pencil?"

"Over there, on that card table, next to my laptop." He'd brought two chairs and a small table into the space that would someday seat restaurant patrons to create a workstation for himself during repairs, though so far, he hadn't spent a single minute in the chair.

Liv handed him the pencil. "Here you go."

She was way too perky. That concerned him too, which was why he had zero intention of asking what she was talking about.

"The roofers will be here on Monday. So don't be alarmed if you hear stomping overhead."

"I won't. Did you hear what I said?" Liv persisted.

"I did, and unless you're ready to let me have the store, we don't have anything to discuss."

"I said I've reconsidered. I think we should share the store."

"You suggested that on Friday. Sharing is not an option."

"Because?"

Sam shook his head. Liv didn't want to hear that smelling her vanilla-and-coconut perfume on a daily basis was not his idea of a good plan. Nope. Running a business with his past was definitely not the way to find his future.

"Because you don't want to work with me," she said.

"Liv, you and I are history. I'm not interested in a business arrangement where we're working together. I'm not even interested in being your landlord, but here we are."

"Yes. Here we are." She nodded. "I have a contract for the entire building, so I guess you'll learn to deal with it."

"I'm going to talk to my lawyer on Monday," he said firmly.

"Seriously, Sam? I'm willing to compromise."

"This isn't personal. Gramps made a mistake leasing both shops. Mistakes happen." Yep, that was the truth. But he didn't intend to let this mistake take his plans for the future from him.

"Oh well, since it isn't personal..."

"Do you smell that?" Sam asked. He looked around unable to quite pinpoint the aroma. A savory, yet earthy scent. Maybe mushrooms? Definitely onions and garlic. His stomach agreed and growled in response.

"Chicken and porcini mushrooms." Liv gave a broad smile. "Smells wonderful, doesn't it?"

"You're cooking?"

"Baking, to be precise." She raised a finger in the air and cocked her head toward the kitchen. "The timer should go off in about two minutes."

Wait… Liv was using the stove. Alarmed, he turned toward her. "I haven't had a plumber evaluate the stove or the ovens. A tornado came through here. I don't know if the gas line is secure."

"You didn't tell me I couldn't cook yet." Hands on her hips, Liv narrowed her eyes. "Do you know how many recipes I need to test? Every oven is different. This is a crucial step for my opening."

Sam climbed down the ladder. "Are you kidding me? You have to turn off the oven until it's been checked."

A buzzer sounded. "Fine." She shrugged. "It's done anyhow."

"Thank you. I know a plumber who owes me a favor. I'll have him out here tomorrow."

"That would be helpful. Thank you." She turned to leave.

"Wait," he called. "Aren't you going to tell me what you're baking?"

"Chicken-and-mushroom potpies. The puff pastry crust is an old recipe. I wasn't sure it would work at this altitude, but it looks perfect. Lightly brown and buttery."

Potpies? He loved potpies.

Sam followed her into the kitchen area, where dirty dishes and pans were stacked on stainless-steel counters. She'd been cooking, that was obvious. He said a silent prayer, thankful that the whole place hadn't ignited.

"What's the plan back here?" he asked.

Liv turned off the industrial oven and opened the door. She smiled serenely and removed two ceramic ramekins with cooking mitts. "Kitchen. Serving line. The usual. I have some design ideas, including painting the walls." She scanned the kitchen. "Obviously, I have to work with the setup here, but that's what I do."

"What you do?" he asked. One glance at

the bubbly, golden-brown potpie had his stomach protesting even louder.

"I'm a restaurant management consultant."

Sam searched her face, confused by the answer. "I thought you were a chef."

"Yes. I have a culinary degree. I've worked in all areas of the restaurant hospitality industry. I sort of stumbled into the consultant job and realized I love telling people what to do."

"A consultant?" All this time, he thought she was cooking in fancy kitchens somewhere.

"Yes." Liv nodded. "My job was to assist start-up restaurants and, more often, save floundering ones. Everything from design to operations, finances, staffing and back-office management." She smiled. "I work with a team and typically bring in a numbers person to handle the finances. That's not my favorite part."

"That's impressive." He couldn't hide the surprise in his voice.

"Is it?"

"Yeah. You gave that up for your father? Does he realize?"

"No. And that information stays in this kitchen." She cocked her head and eyed him. "Besides, I don't see it as giving up anything. Running my own restaurant has always been my goal, and I'm pursuing it."

His dream was up against her dream. That was the bottom line here. Sam couldn't help frowning as he stared at her.

"What?" she asked. "If you've got something to say, say it."

"Hard to believe you aspire to start a restaurant here. New York City or Denver, maybe. But Homestead Pass?" He was certain his face reflected how skeptical he was of the whole situation.

"You can scoff all you want. But one thing I've learned is that location doesn't matter. Or how you pivot or compromise to accomplish your goals. All that matters is that I'm going to finally reach mine."

Sam blinked, considering her words.

He'd been dabbling with wood since he was a kid, watching his father cut and plane wood. Being in the workshop stirred up those good memories. Yet it was practicality that stood in the way of chasing the dream of becoming a full-time craftsman. The Lazy M required all the Morgan boys after his parents passed.

Then when it turned out he could make a lucrative living crunching numbers, he'd become the ranch accountant and picked up other customers as well.

How had he gotten so off course?

Liv was resolute about getting what she wanted, no matter the circumstance. Maybe he could learn from her example.

She opened the stainless-steel, monster refrigerator and took out a bag of greens.

"What are you making now?" His stomach continued to grumble as the savory aromas reminded him lunch was well over six hours ago.

"Just a salad to go with the meal."

"Do you need a taste tester?" he asked.

Liv looked at him and laughed. The sound of her laughter brought back memories he'd buried. They used to enjoy each other's company.

"Sure," she said. "Why not?"

His gaze followed her as she moved efficiently around the kitchen, pulling plates and silverware from industrial metal shelves.

"Where do you want to eat?" she asked.

"Card table." Sam quickly cleared off his laptop and paperwork before she changed her mind.

Liv placed two plates with large pastry-topped ramekins on the table, along with a serving bowl with the salad, then looked at him. "I hope you like pear-and-Gorgonzola vinaigrette on spring greens."

"I never met a food I didn't like." He took the silverware from her hands and finished setting their impromptu dinner table.

"All I have on hand is water."

"Water is great. This is great. I'm starving." He sat down and unfolded his napkin. "Did you plan to invite me to eat?"

"No, you invited yourself. I was testing the oven. The recipe makes two potpies. I would have eaten both of them if you weren't here."

At least she was honest. He nodded.

"Looks like I'm finally in the right place at the right time."

Liv smiled. "Let's pray." She bowed her head but didn't reach for his hand. "Thank you, Lord, for this food. Bless it to our bodies and bless our endeavors in this building. Amen."

"Amen."

They ate in silence until Liv put down her fork and looked at him. "Well, you haven't said anything."

No, he hadn't. He was too busy eating and thinking. It had been a long time since he and Liv had sat at a table across from each other. The last time, her engagement ring sparkled on her left hand. If anyone had told him they'd be sitting in the Snodgrass Building today, eating the best potpie he'd ever had in his life, well, he'd be certain they were joking.

"I didn't say anything because I figured I'd better eat this before you changed your mind and snatched it away."

Liv smiled, her dark eyes sparkling. Cooking was what made her happy. That's what she should be doing, not consulting. He hoped she realized that.

"Best meal I've ever had." Sam paused. "I've had your cooking before, and it was good. This is next level. Nuanced. Your restaurant is bound to be a success."

"That's very generous of you to say. Thank you."

"It's the truth." He chased a pea around his plate with a fork. "Though I'd appreciate it if you didn't tell Bess."

She grinned. "What's said in the kitchen stays in the kitchen."

"Glad to hear it. Though I'm not convinced your store will be viable."

"If that's your spiel to convince me to give up the shop, forget it," she huffed. "Besides, I see overlap in your business and mine. Cutting boards are definitely kitchen goods."

"True, though my designs are more rustic, and the price tag is...excuse the pun, palatable. This is Homestead Pass. You can't charge city prices in a small town." Sam raised a shoulder.

"Excuse me?" Liv's voice reflected her outrage.

"I do have experience with small businesses," he continued. "I've done the books or the taxes for half the businesses on Main Street. I've seen them open and close."

She exhaled slowly, her expression telling him exactly what she thought of his opinion. That was too bad, because he did have a knowledge base when it came to what survived and thrived in this particular town. If they didn't have a history, Liv might be more receptive to his words.

"What's your point, Sam? I mean other than being a buzzkill."

"My point is that you've been gone a long time. You know restaurants, but I don't think you understand the clientele that purchases in this town. Locals and tourists."

"Once again, I disagree."

"We can put it to the test." He leaned back in his chair as an idea began to percolate. For a second, he wondered if she had put something in his food because he couldn't believe what he was about to suggest.

"I don't like that look in your eyes. What are you up to?"

"Maybe we can find out whose merchandise sells better. Yours or mine."

"I don't follow."

"What about a field inventory survey? Say…six weeks? Starting with the Memorial Day crowd. That will take us right up to the week of the Fourth of July. Whoever generates the most sales takes over the shop."

A brilliant plan, if he did say so himself.

"Interesting bargain, cowboy, but I already paid a year's rent," she returned with a shrug.

"I'll reimburse you when I outsell you."

Liv choked back a laugh. "No lack of arrogance in your back pocket, huh, Morgan?"

"Not at all. I simply have confidence that the folks of Homestead Pass will be eager to purchase handcrafted wood products. Trust me. My products will fly off the shelves." Even as he said the words, excitement began to build. It occurred to him that Liv renting the space he wanted had kicked him out of his complacency. He was finally going after his own dream, and it felt good. Sam smiled at the thought, then resumed a serious expression. He could grin after he'd closed the gate on this deal.

"Fly off the shelves? That's a lofty statement," she leaned across the table and raised a hand in gesture. "Do you even have the inventory for such an ambitious endeavor?"

Sam gave a slow head shake. The less he said, the better. He knew too well how competitive Liv was. She was almost at yes.

"No need to concern yourself with my inventory," he finally said.

"Sam, you have no idea what you're up against."

"Does that mean you're interested in this opportunity?" Again, he worked to remain casual, hoping to lure her right in.

She pushed her plate aside and rested her chin on her folded hands. "I don't understand why you would suggest such an arrangement when you're so adamant about not working with me."

"We won't be working together. I have no plans to participate in the management of the shop. I can even plan to deliver my inventory after hours."

"I'm tempted to trounce you on principle."

"Then, say yes."

She frowned. "I'd need to find a good numbers person. Someone who can track the separate sales."

He chuckled and pointed to himself. "You're looking at the best numbers person in the area. Hire an experienced store manager to oversee inventory. I'll handle the finances."

"Why would you offer to do that?"

"Because I'm the best person for the job." He smiled. "This plan nets you a free accountant temporarily. Just have your store manager mail the receipts to my post office box once a week."

She appeared to consider the idea. "And you don't mind that townsfolk will think... you and I?" Her face pinked at the question.

"They won't think anything." Once again, he slowly shook his head, making it clear that was the last thing he wanted. "I have a day job at Lazy M Ranch, so I don't see our paths crossing."

Liv was silent for minutes, her dark brows knit together in thought. "Hmm."

"Hmm, what?"

"Aside from the fact that you've insulted me again, it's a reasonable plan."

Reasonable? It was a brilliant plan. The shop would be his by the end of summer.

"What if I'm asked about the products?" Liv asked.

"A local craftsman will be your answer."

Liv stared at him intently. "Tell me again why you're doing this?"

Sam leaned across the table and met her gaze. He was absolutely serious now.

"Because I want that shop."

Liv Moretti wasn't the only one with something to prove. He wanted something that was his, and he'd always known deep down inside that what he crafted with his heart and his hands was his future.

Liv's eyes widened at his words.

"You asked." Sam shrugged and leaned back again. "Now, do we have a deal?"

"Six weeks. Starting Memorial Day weekend."

"Yep."

"What if my landlord doesn't have repairs done by then?"

"He will."

"Okay then, I agree to your limited-time arrangement with the terms as previously discussed."

Sam held out a hand, and she offered hers. For a moment, he stared at their joined hands. This was either the smartest thing he'd ever done or the dumbest. He was about to find out.

Chapter Four

"**W**as that the doorbell?" Sam looked at Lucas across the kitchen table. His brother's short caramel-colored hair was wet and slicked back. He'd showered twice today. A sure sign that he had a date.

"Yep. Sounded like a doorbell to me." Lucas finished off his soda and reached for another slice of pizza.

"Don't get up or anything," Sam said.

"It's your house."

"You live here."

"Not for long."

Sam stared, amazed, as his brother folded his slice in half and practically downed the pizza in one bite. He was definitely eating for two, himself and his impressive biceps. Moving hay for the last few months did that to a guy.

"Not for long? What's that supposed to mean?" Sam asked.

Lucas finished chewing and wiped his mouth with a napkin. "I'm moving out. Gotta get my things to the main house before I leave on Friday. The first rodeo of the season is coming up. I told you all this."

"Refresh my memory."

"Drew and Sadie and the baby moved out of the main house into their new one last month and Gramps is alone. An eighty-one-year-old man shouldn't be living by himself. I'm moving in with him. Trevor is too."

"Oh?" Sam perked at that news. While he loved his younger brothers, living with them was like living in a frat house. They redefined the word *slob*—especially Lucas. And he wasn't keen on spending his time mothering them. If they moved in with their grandfather, Bess would keep them in line, and they could keep Gramps in line.

"Try not to look so happy," Lucas said. "If you wanted to get rid of us, you should have said something sooner."

"It's not you that I want to get rid of," Sam said. "It's your boxes in my workshop." The timing was perfect. Now he could augment his inventory for the shop he planned to take over from Liv at the end of summer.

"Those aren't my boxes. They belong to Trevor. All my stuff is in my trailer. Besides, I don't see what a big deal it is. It's not like you're ever here anyhow. I've hardly seen you at all this past week. I thought you moved out."

Sam blinked. "I've been at the Snodgrass Building when I wasn't at the ranch." It had been over a week since the tornado hit and he hadn't made enough progress to ensure Liv would be in business by Memorial Day.

Trevor clomped into the kitchen a moment later and dropped to a chair.

"Did you get the door?" Sam asked Trevor.

"No. It's your house."

Sam released a disgusted huff but didn't move from his seat. If he abandoned his slice of pizza, it would be gone when he returned.

"What were you two arguing about?" Trevor asked.

"Just telling Sam that we're moving out," Lucas responded.

"I'm still not sure moving out is such a good idea," Trevor said to Lucas. He grabbed a slice of pizza.

"Reason number one. The main house is closer to Bess's cooking," Lucas said. "Reason number two. Refer to reason number one."

"There is that," Trevor said. "Her cooking sure beats ours." He gestured toward Lucas with the wedge of pizza in his hand. "You're heading out this week?"

"Friday."

"This your last season?" Trevor returned.

Lucas jerked back at the words, his eyes rounding. "Are you calling me old?"

"No. I'm asking if this is your last season. We could use you on the ranch. With Drew cutting back hours since the baby was born and Sam riding a desk, I need more full-time wranglers."

"I'm not retiring. I'll be thirty-five at the end of the season. That is *not* old." He looked at Sam and cocked his head toward Trevor. "Tell him."

"Tell him, nothing," Sam scoffed. "Thirty-five is old for a cowboy on the circuit. I retired at thirty-two, and I sure wasn't putting in as many miles as you. I had to help Drew with the ranch pretty much full-time after college. I was only working local rodeos."

"That's not my fault," Lucas said.

"You're missing the point, Junior. The only reason to continue is if you like sleeping standing up, drinking burnt coffee, and nursing cracked ribs and a concussion." He raised his palms. "But, hey, you keep riding those broncs. Not too long, and you'll be eligible for the National Senior Pro Rodeo Association."

Trevor snorted at the words.

"Thanks for the support." Lucas scowled and left the room.

A loud banging on the front door had Sam shoving the rest of his pizza into his mouth and jumping from his seat. He stomped to the door and yanked it open. Drew stood on the porch.

"Your doorbell doesn't work."

"Oh, it works. I figured if I didn't answer, you might go away." Sam eyed Drew before he turned away, leaving his brother to close the door. The guy was always smiling these days. It had started when Sadie agreed to marry him, and he hadn't stopped since. It was getting annoying.

"You're in a good mood," Drew called out.

Sam kept walking. "I didn't order enough pizza for a family reunion."

"I already ate dinner."

"Then, why are you here?"

"I brought an apple pie from Bess, but I can leave if you prefer."

At that, Sam stopped and turned around. He took the warm container from Drew's hands and smiled. Just looking at the crisscrossed golden crust covering apples nestled in a pale brown caramel sauce did his heart good after the day he'd had.

"I also stopped by for a chat with you and the boys," Drew said.

As the oldest sibling, Drew referred to the twins as "the boys." A habit left over from the years after their parents died when he'd helped Gramps raise them.

"They're here, all right." Sam eyed his brother with suspicion. "A chat?"

"Relax. I'll only be here a few minutes. Then you can get back to being a cranky old man."

Sam placed the pie on the table and eased into his chair once again. "I'm not cranky. I'm tired. Only got home an hour ago."

Drew gave Trevor a nod and glanced around. "Where's Luc?"

"Upstairs, getting ready for a date. He'll be back down when he smells that pie." Trevor got up and fumbled in the kitchen drawers until he found a knife and a pie spatula. "Was there a reason you brought this bribe? Not that I'm complaining."

"It's not a bribe. Bess sent it over." Drew

opened the refrigerator and did a double take as he grabbed a cola. "Bess made you a cake. She sure has been busy."

"It's tiramisu, not cake." Sam wasn't going to tell him that Bess wasn't responsible for the cocoa-covered confection in his fridge. Liv had insisted he take home half of the test dessert she'd made in the restaurant today.

If there were a perk to having her around irritating him, it would be the food. Ever since the plumber gave the okay on the stove, Liv had been baking and cooking nonstop. Testing, she called it. He called it lunch and dinner.

"Tiramisu. That's Italian, isn't it?" Drew gave a slow nod of understanding as he met Sam's gaze.

"I guess so," Sam murmured. He took a swig of soda and ignored his brother.

Drew chuckled and kept talking. "I hear you've been meeting yourself coming and going. Cleaning up that tornado mess, working on that building and helping Trev with ranch chores."

"Is our new ranch manager complaining?" Sam turned to look at Trevor.

"I'd never complain behind your back." Trevor's fork hovered over the slice of pie in front of him. "Especially when I can do it to your face."

Sam glared at Drew. "I'm right on schedule with the ranch books, and I've picked up some chores when I can. I don't see that there's a problem."

"No problem. I'm concerned about you," Drew said. "You all helped me step back from managing the ranch when I got married. I figured maybe there's a way we can help you."

"What's the plan with that building?" Trevor asked around a mouthful of pie.

"The plan is that I'm on a tight deadline. I've got until Memorial Day left to complete repairs." Sam released a breath of frustration. "Sooner, actually, so Liv can prep the restaurant and shop for the opening."

"How did you get yourself in this fix?" Drew asked.

"He can't say no." Lucas strode into the

room carrying a wicker laundry basket overflowing with dirty clothes.

"This isn't about saying no," Sam shot back.

"Then, what is it about? Boundaries, maybe?" Lucas dropped the basket on the floor.

"Where are you going with your laundry?" Trevor asked. "I thought you had a date."

"I do. First I'm stopping at the main house to drop this off. I cut a deal with Bess. If I give her a hand in the garden, she'll do my wash."

Trevor eyed the basket. "Does she know you haven't done laundry in a month?"

"She didn't ask."

"Hello? Can we focus here?" Drew asked. "Have a seat, Luc."

"Yes, sir." He gave a mock salute before he straddled a kitchen chair backward.

Drew turned back to Sam. "Seems you're spending all your time at the Snodgrass Building. What's going on with you and Olivia?"

Sam stiffened at the question. He was

weary of explaining himself to the world. Olivia Moretti was history. Period. Thankfully, the repairs were almost done, and soon his days would no longer be bound to a woman who saw him as a two-dimensional cardboard cowboy. A woman who still held the power to break his heart.

"Me and Olivia?" he finally responded. "Not a thing. It's purely a business arrangement."

The expressions on his brothers' faces said that not one of them believed him.

"Look, I'm not happy about the situation," Sam said. "But I'm her landlord, thanks to Gramps." He paused. "I don't want you to say anything to him. It was an honest mistake."

"And..." Drew prodded.

"I'm stuck. As such, I have a legal obligation to repair the tornado damage to the Snodgrass Building. She signed the contract while I was out of town and paid a year's rent." He narrowed his gaze. "Any more questions?"

"Can't you outsource?" Trevor asked.

"Outsourcing isn't cheap. I mailed in

photos and estimates after I talked to the insurance company. They're backed up during tornado season. I don't expect a check anytime soon." He shrugged. "Besides, I'm not the only business hit by that twister. We're all trying to get repairs done at the same time. That's slowing things down as well."

"How can we help?" Drew asked.

He appreciated that his brothers were willing to step up, but they had their own busy lives. "I can't ask you to help again. You all lost a Saturday to storm cleanup."

"We're family." Drew looked at Trevor and Lucas, who both nodded.

Trevor gestured toward Lucas. "Put him to work. He's gone come Friday, but that gives you a couple of days."

"You okay with that, Lucas?" Sam asked.

His brother shrugged. "Sure. I could use a reprieve from calf birthing."

"I can give you some hours on Saturday," Trevor said.

"Same here," Drew added. "I'm yours all day Saturday."

Sam leaned back in his chair, considering. "That would be great. I've got a list a mile long of things you fellas can do."

"All right." Drew nodded. "Sounds like a plan to me."

Sam's cell phone rang, and he pulled it out of his pocket without looking at the caller ID. "Morgan."

"Sam, I saw a mouse."

Liv.

He got up and stepped into the hallway so his brothers wouldn't overhear. After all, he'd only minutes ago assured him that he had boundaries in place. "And you're calling me. Why?"

"I said, I saw a mouse in my restaurant!"

"Okay. Okay. Calm down."

"Don't tell me to calm down." Her voice inched up a decibel. "I don't think you understand the implications here. The health department could shut the place down before it opens."

He looked at his watch. "It's after five. I'll reach out to someone in the morning... Why are you still there?"

"I'm working. The question you should

be asking is how could this have happened?"

Sam tensed. He glanced over his shoulder and stepped farther into the hallway. "I'm happy to handle the situation tomorrow."

There was a long silence.

"You can't talk?" she asked.

"That's right."

"Fine. Tomorrow. Tell the exterminator to park near the inn and enter the restaurant through the back door. This needs to be handled with discretion."

"I can do that."

"Tomorrow, Sam. I want someone here tomorrow. I have food deliveries coming on Wednesday, and I do not want to think about a mouse in my supplies."

"Thanks for calling."

"What?"

He disconnected the phone and stepped back into the kitchen. All three of his brothers stared at him with know-it-all smirks. All he could do was shake his head.

"Who was that?" Lucas asked.

"Business."

Trevor eyed him. "She sure was yelling her business loud."

Drew sputtered, nearly choking on his soda before he released a belly laugh. Sam rubbed the bridge of his nose. "I told you. I'm her landlord. There's not much I can do about the situation."

"Seems like Miss Olivia has you on a short leash, Mr. Landlord," Lucas returned with a laugh.

Yeah, Lucas was right. She did. End of the month couldn't get here soon enough.

Sam shook his head. Life sure had been a lot simpler before Olivia Moretti came back to town.

Liv grimaced at the creak of the cupboard door. One day she'd fix those hinges. They had been giving away her food raids in the family kitchen since she was a child.

She pulled out the peanut butter and placed it on the kitchen counter, along with a jar of honey.

"Is that you, Olivia?"

"*Sì*, Zia," Liv answered her Aunt Loretta in Italian as she quickly prepared her breakfast and slid it into a paper bag.

Her aunt appeared in the kitchen a moment later. Even at 5:00 a.m., Loretta glowed in a red silk kimono. She ran her fingers through her disheveled black hair with its strategic silver highlights and yawned.

Liv's heart swelled as she looked at her aunt. After the very lucrative sale of her New York City bistro, Loretta Moretti had spent time flitting around the globe. A year ago, she'd landed in Homestead Pass where she taught cooking classes, dabbled in catering and kept an eye on Liv's father.

Loretta's arrival blessed the entire Moretti household and Liv was grateful.

"Zia, how is it you look so good so early in the morning?"

"Do I?"

"Yes. It's disgusting." Liv slathered peanut butter and honey on homemade bread and cut the sandwich in half.

Loretta laughed. Then she reached for the stove-top espresso maker and added water and coffee before placing it on a burner. "Where are you going so early? The sun isn't even up yet."

"I've got a big delivery for the restaurant this morning and one for goods store in the afternoon."

Loretta turned on the burner. "I heard a rumor that there was an exterminator truck in the parking lot next to your building yesterday."

Liv cringed and kept her head down as she washed an apple. "Hmm. I wonder what that was about?"

"I don't know." Loretta opened the refrigerator and took out half of the tiramisu that Liv had brought home on Monday. "This is excellent, by the way. New recipe?"

"No. I tweaked Nonna's recipe. Now it's *Americano.*"

"Don't tell your father."

"Never," Liv said. Her father believed that the recipes handed down from his mother were sacred. Not a single ingredient should be altered. What he didn't know would keep peace in the kitchen.

Loretta cut herself a square and took

a small bite. *"Bellissima."* She offered a chef's kiss.

"You're having tiramisu for breakfast?" Liv laughed.

"Sure. Why not?" Loretta smiled. "How are things going at the restaurant?"

"Fine. Just fine." *Overwhelming* was more like it. Instead of panicking, Liv focused on the positive. May was a long month, and there were two-and-a-half weeks left until the opening of her restaurant. Until then, she'd continue to prep for the launch by working from dawn until dusk. Dreams didn't come without a price tag.

"When's your soft launch?"

"The Thursday before Memorial Day Weekend," Liv squeaked.

"What?" Loretta's mouth opened in exclamation. "Is that realistic? You know the big Homestead Pass Spring Dance is Friday. I'll be busy catering the event, so I can't offer my assistance until after the dance."

Liv nodded. "The official opening isn't until Saturday."

"Still. You could use some help, Olivia."

"I have help. Do you remember my friend Robyn from culinary college?"

"From Oklahoma City? Yes. You two were trouble together as I recall."

Liv laughed. The story of their science lab disaster had been exaggerated.

"Why do you mention Robyn?"

"I've hired her in the past to help with kitchen management renovations. She's agreed to spend the summer in Homestead Pass as sous-chef. That will take the pressure off me. She arrives Sunday night."

Loretta tilted her head. "Still, she's not in the kitchen yet."

"Robyn has the menus and we've been video cooking for weeks."

"Video cooking?" Her aunt's brow rose. "Is that a thing?"

"It is now. We review the menu, schedule the video chat and cook together."

Loretta mumbled a few choice words in Italian.

"Zia, I had to be creative for this to work."

"That's creative, all right. Tell me more about your plans."

"The menu is set. Dinner only, to start, though I am considering a weekend brunch in the future." She paused. "The local vendors are lined up, contracts signed."

"Staff?"

She grinned. "Yes. I've hired experienced waitstaff and porters."

"And Robyn. Will she be staying with us?"

Liv nodded. "I'll put her in the guest cottage." While there was plenty of room in the family quarters to house her friend for the summer, the cottage would afford her privacy.

"Wonderful. I'll prepare the cottage."

"Oh, Zia. That would be so helpful. Thank you."

"How else may I assist?"

"I haven't made a final decision on the seating chart for the restaurant. The furniture arrives tomorrow." Liv was excited about the tables and chairs she'd purchased from a restaurant outlet in Oklahoma City. "Once I have everything set up, I'd be grateful if you could spend time at each table and let me know what you think. You know..." She raised her hands. "The usual. Drafts, sun glare, noise from the kitchen, odors."

"I'd be delighted to play disgruntled customer and find something wrong with your seating arrangement."

"You're a lifesaver." She reached out to hug her aunt. The woman was both mother and sister, and Liv relied on her wisdom often.

"What about your father's grumbling? Do you have a plan for that as well?" Liv asked.

Liv put her sandwich inside the paper bag and closed the top. "What's he grumbling about now?"

"He's unhappy that you're spending so much time in town."

"So much time in town? My business is in town. I never miss Sunday supper, do I?" She groaned. "I take him to all his physician appointments. There's no pleasing him."

"The man needs something to do," Loretta said.

"He has a ranch." Liv waved a hand toward the window and its view of Angus cattle grazing.

"If you recall, the doctor benched him. Even horseback riding is off the table for now." Her aunt shrugged. "Besides, M&M runs itself. Anthony has a competent ranch manager who does everything except sign the checks these days."

"This makes no sense. Why doesn't my father sell the ranch?"

"Ah, Olivia. He doesn't sell because Anthony Moretti built this place from nothing, and he hasn't given up hope that you'll marry and take over his legacy. You know your father. He's dropped the lyrics to that old song more than a few times since you've been gone and since you've returned." Loretta sighed. "I feel for him. *La famiglia* is everything, and he wants M&M Ranch to pass on to his children."

"Me. I'm it." Liv bemoaned being an only child. It meant that the burden of her father's expectations fell directly on her shoulders.

Loretta raised her brows and pointed a finger. "Yes. So you must talk to him." She turned at the spitting and hissing of the espresso maker, took it off the stove and poured the dark brew into a cup.

"I have, Zia." Liv recalled apologizing to her father for the expense he'd incurred because she canceled the wedding. She vowed to pay him back, and she had. Money he understood.

As for her dreams? No amount of heartfelt explanations could get through to him. He'd built the ranch for his descendants and Liv was supposed to fall in line with the plan.

"Try again, Olivia. Make sure he's actually listening."

"Ugh." Liv paused. "Then he'll hand me a boarding pass for a first-class guilt trip." She shook her head. "I'm doing my best to postpone that trip for now. Thank you very much."

Loretta nodded her head slowly and sighed. "Guilt. The gift that keeps on giving. Eventually, you're going to have to dig deep and find the courage to stand up for yourself."

Liv sighed. Each time she thought the

situation was resolved, her father carried on as though they'd never discussed her lack of interest in managing the ranch.

"I know. I know," she said. "Just not today."

"Fine. We won't speak of it again." Loretta patted Liv's arm. "Tell me more about what's going on with your restaurant. Am I invited to the soft launch?"

"Absolutely."

"I won't go easy on you."

"Good. I want the hard truth."

"I agree." Loretta sipped her espresso. "What about your home goods store?"

"Thankfully, that's under control. There's no shortage of college students in the area to staff the store. I hired three gals yesterday. And I've hired a retired school librarian as the manager."

"Sounds like you're very organized."

"I'm a little nervous because at this point, if one thing goes awry, it will domino, and I'll be in trouble."

She wiped down the counter, mulling the situation. It was possible that she'd bit off more than she should have. Her original plan was to open a home goods store after the restaurant had established a rhythm. But when she saw both spaces were empty, she jumped right in and began ordering merchandise. That was even before Sam had showed up with his objections. Now there was no turning back.

"What's your vision for the store?" Loretta asked.

She looked at her aunt, who seemed to be reading her mind.

"My mother used to take me to home goods shops in Oklahoma City and Tulsa." Liv smiled as tender pangs of nostalgia had her thoughts slipping back to the past. She missed those jaunts. "It seemed a tribute to her to open a store like that here," Liv continued.

"Then why the worried face?" her aunt asked. "Are you second-guessing yourself?"

"Absolutely." Liv laughed.

"I have the utmost confidence in you, Olivia."

"I feel the same about you, Zia. I'm hoping that you're still thinking about moving your classes and catering from the inn into the restaurant."

"I don't want to get in your way."

"You won't. There's a huge office and an extra room behind the prep kitchen." Liv smiled. "Just think about it."

"I will. I'm excited about the idea."

"Good." Liv checked her watch. "Uh-oh. Time to run."

Thirty minutes later, she pulled up in front of the Snodgrass Building and parked her father's truck. The rising sun bathed the brick building in a pink glow. Streetlamps seemed to spotlight the newly installed signs—Moretti's Farm-to-Table Bistro and The Inspired Kitchen.

Giddy with pleasure, Liv hugged herself. She was still grinning as she got out of the truck and glanced about.

She tiptoed around the orange cones on the sidewalk where workers had poured concrete to repair the damage from the uprooted redbud. Unlocking the door to the restaurant, she turned on the lights and stood at the threshold as though she were a customer. The newly refinished oak floors sparkled. Her gaze went to the walls, now coated in green earth tones that complemented the exposed brick on the other side of the room. Sam had been generous in offering to repaint everything since he had to plaster the damaged walls and cover those areas anyhow.

For a grumbling and cranky landlord, he'd done right by her. She couldn't be more pleased and couldn't wait for the painting to be completed in the shop too.

"The Inspired Kitchen? What kind of name is that?" Liv whirled around to see Sam getting out of his truck. "You might have consulted me since I'm going to be the new owner in a few months."

"Dream on." She peered up and down the street, hoping that no one had overheard him, but the town hadn't woken yet. "And it's a lovely name."

"Lovely?" Sam chuckled and adjusted the ball cap on his head.

"Yes. Everyone has a kitchen, and my shop will inspire them."

"Our shop," he returned.

"The restaurant looks wonderful," she said, ignoring his comment and avoiding looking directly at him. Sam was remarkably handsome so early in the morning. He didn't even have bedhead.

"We can agree on that. And the insurance company approved the claim. Which means your landlord will be reimbursed soon."

"Wonderful. What about the walls of the shop?"

"Lucas will be here through Thursday. That will expedite those repairs. Then Trevor and Drew will paint on Saturday. We're in the home stretch. Mostly small things on the to-do list."

"That's wonderful."

"Don't get too excited. I'm still waiting on the county to send someone out to sign off on the HVAC installation."

Liv stepped into the restaurant, and Sam followed.

"What about you?" he asked. "Weren't

you doing some renovations in the rest-rooms?"

"Yes. A facelift to match the dining area update. Sinks and commodes. I talked to the plumber on Monday when he was here. He wants a small fortune. It will have to wait."

"Do you have the supplies?" Sam asked.

"They arrived yesterday."

"Lucas is very handy. He can do that for you. Just slip him a nice tip."

Liv brightened at his words. "Really?"

Sam nodded. "He's leaving for the rodeo on Friday. A little cash will come in handy."

"Oh, thank you. I really appreciate that." Liv peeked at him, surprised at the gesture of goodwill.

"No problem. The sooner we get things tied up here, the sooner I can get back to my regularly scheduled life."

"Right. Yes. Of course." Once again, she was reminded that Sam was here because he had to be. Not by choice. The only way they could return to the easy friendship of the past was if she shared what was in the letter he'd tossed years ago.

He deserved a face-to-face explanation. Now all she had to do was find the courage to do that.

Chapter Five

"Hey, Olivia, can you take a look at the front door? The second coat is dry." Lucas stood just inside the kitchen.

"Sure." Liv pulled off her apron and quickly followed him through the restaurant to the sidewalk. "That color is perfect." She eyed the burgundy paint she'd chosen from all angles and grinned.

"Think two coats is enough?" he asked.

"I do."

"Great. I'll add some varnish next. It's taking forever to dry in this humidity, but I've got to have ventilation." He shrugged. "It will be ready to put back on its hinges before you close up tonight."

"Thank you so much, Lucas." She examined the door, which rested against the building on a tarp. Front door painted. Check. Each step completed brought her closer to her plans for the future coming true. "Funny how such a small thing makes me deliriously happy."

"The women I date want horses and tickets to a country music concert. Here you are, tickled over doors."

"Perhaps you're dating the wrong women." Liv stepped back into the restaurant, and he followed.

"I won't rule that out. I've been known to fall for a gal based on how much she gushes over my standings on the leaderboard."

Liv bit her lip, working not to laugh. "Thanks again, Lucas."

"Sure. Oh, and those bathroom fixtures? I'll have the install completed this afternoon."

"Really?" Her brows shot up at his words. "That fast. I am so appreciative."

"Hey, I'm appreciative of the gourmet meals you've been feeding me." He grinned and nodded toward the kitchen. "I'll miss them when I leave tomorrow. I wouldn't mind working for you full-time."

"You'd hate being indoors every single day, and I'm sure you'd miss the rodeo."

"Maybe." Lucas shrugged. "Though my brothers are all harassing me about retiring."

She cocked her head and looked at him. For once, the cowboy wasn't laughing. "What do you want to do?"

"I'm not sure. Last year was a really good year. Maybe I should quit while I'm on top."

"Have you given any thought to the future?"

"Oh yeah. Sure. When I do, if I do, I'd like to open a bronc riding school on the ranch."

"I'm intrigued."

"You're intrigued, and I'm scared," he said. Lucas met her gaze, and she saw the vulnerability in his blue eyes.

"Don't they say that the best dreams should scare us?"

Lucas removed his ball cap and slapped

it back on with a self-deprecating smile. "If that's the case, I can admit I'm terrified."

"Why? You're qualified. And as I recall, you have a business degree under your belt. You have every tool necessary to succeed."

"I don't know. My brothers are tough acts to follow."

"Don't compare yourself to your brothers. Their dreams aren't yours. And no one can tell you what your dreams are." Liv found herself getting worked up as she spoke. "You have to go after what you want."

"Thanks, Olivia. I appreciate hearing that." He turned away and then looked back hesitantly. "Is that why you left Sam? To follow your dream?"

"I..." Liv grimaced and searched for an easy answer. There wasn't one. Yes, she did leave to follow her dream, but the way she went about it was all wrong. Older and wiser didn't excuse her behavior or diminish the pain she'd caused Sam.

Lucas raised a hand. "Don't answer that. I shouldn't have asked. It's none of my business."

"In all honesty, I was a mess five years ago. Did I make the best decisions? Not at all. I am certain that I did the best I could with where I was spiritually and emotionally."

"Fair enough."

"Yoo-hoo!"

The familiar greeting from Mrs. Pickett had Lucas offering a quick salute before he disappeared.

A moment later, the bookstore owner peeked her silver-blond head into the restaurant. "Anyone home?" She read the wet-paint sign before carefully stepping inside.

"Mrs. Pickett," Liv said. "How nice to see you."

"You as well, dear. How are you?" She glanced around the restaurant. "Oh, this is going to be lovely. Look at those table linens. Very elegant. We don't have anything like this in Homestead Pass. I'm sure you're going to be very successful."

"Thank you. I appreciate that."

"It's the truth." She smiled. "I can see you're busy, and I don't want to take up your time. I'm here to formally invite you to the Homestead Pass Business Association meeting. You should have gotten an email invitation and information about annual dues. The meeting is tonight."

Liv pressed her fingers against her mouth. The business meeting. She'd forgotten and now her prep schedule was completely packed.

The bookstore owner cocked her head, waiting for an answer.

"Yes, ma'am. I received the email. However, I'm not certain I'll be able to attend."

"Is it the dues? They cover our joint promotional initiatives during the year, along with a tasty supper provided at quarterly meetings."

"Oh, that's not it." Liv hesitated for a moment. "My schedule in the restaurant…"

"You should make time. The support system and resources provided by the other small business owners is important. Besides, we're all thrilled to have you."

"Really?" Liv had hoped to find a place for herself in Homestead Pass and prayed that her history with Sam wouldn't stand in the way.

"Absolutely," Mrs. Pickett continued. "The meeting is held at the inn. Thankfully, the meeting room was undamaged by the tornado." A smile touched her lips. "Oh, and we have an excellent buffet. In fact, your aunt is responsible for the menu. She always attends our meetings."

"I had no idea."

"Oh, yes. She insisted upon handling the buffet. I believe it had something to do with the rubber chicken the inn usually serves for such events."

"That sounds like Aunt Loretta." Liv laughed. "All right, since my aunt will be there, I will too."

"I don't suppose your father might be interested in attending. I ran into him at the grocery store last week, and we had a lovely chat about pasta of all things." She grinned, her eyes brightening and a hint of pink touching her cheeks. "I didn't even think to ask about the meeting."

"My father?" Liv asked.

"Yes, he used to attend regularly. Of course, that was before he lost your mother, and I lost my dear husband."

"I didn't realize that you were widowed. I'm so sorry."

"Oh, my dear, it's been nearly ten years, but thank you. Now, don't forget to speak to your father. I'm sure he'll enjoy himself."

"I'll certainly ask him."

"Thank you." Her grin grew even wider, leaving Liv to wonder if Mrs. Pickett could be interested in her father.

The idea shook her for a moment. Then she realized it might be an inspired idea for her father to find interests outside of the ranch and nagging her.

"It would mean so much to the old-timers to see him there," Mrs. Pickett continued. "You know, your father used to advocate for the other ranchers in town. He never missed a meeting or an event."

"You're right." Liv recalled her father's community activism when she was growing up. "Thank you for that reminder. I'll call him right away."

"Wonderful. Oh, and while I'm here." Mrs. Pickett dug in her purse and pulled out a large manila envelope. "The association has one of our big fundraisers coming up the Friday of Memorial Day weekend. The annual Homestead Pass Spring Dance. The local businesses are closing early on Friday to encourage everyone to attend the dance."

"Yes. I know." Liv nodded. The dance was the reason her restaurant was officially opening on Saturday. There was no point competing with an event catered by her aunt.

The woman cocked her head. "I didn't see your name on the list of attendees."

"I…" Liv again found herself short an answer. She was buried with prep for the restaurant and the shop. How could she take time to attend a dance?

"This year it will benefit our health clinic." Mrs. Pickett continued. "You can't go wrong to pick up one for yourself and another for a plus-one." She raised her brows suggestively. "As I said, it's for a good cause."

Liv recognized a professional. The woman had taken guilt lessons from her father. She may as well concede now, or she'd never get back to the kitchen. After all, Robyn was coming to town and might enjoy the event.

"Sure, Mrs. Pickett. I'll take two."

"Fabulous." Mrs. Pickett concluded the transaction and offered a finger wave as she headed out the door.

Liv stared at the tickets in her hand. Her father attending a dance would be a reach. But inviting him to the small business meeting was a great idea. Liv needed to get her father involved in something besides complaining about what the doctor said he couldn't do. This was exactly what he needed.

And probably what she needed as well. It was time to network with the other business owners. The dance? That would depend on how tonight went.

She pulled out her cell phone and tapped in her father's number. "Papà, would you like to attend the small business meeting with me tonight?"

"Why would I do that?"

Liv palmed her forehead. "Because I invited you. I thought it might be nice for us to do something together."

Liv could practically hear the wheels going in his head and prepared for his refusal.

"Mrs. Pickett asked about you. She'll be there."

"She will?" More silence.

"Papà?"

"I guess I could check it out. I haven't been in years." He paused. "We'll go together?"

"Yes. That's what I said. I'll finish up here and come home and pick you up."

Liv glanced at her watch. She had better hustle.

Several hours later, she glanced at her watch again as she stepped into the inn's banquet room with her father. He had hounded her from the moment she'd arrived home to shower and change.

"Morettis are never late," he called as she blow-dried her hair.

They arrived at the meeting right on time, only to have her father grumble as his gaze assessed the attendees.

"Same crowd. They've just gotten older."

"Papà. You haven't been here in how many years?"

He shrugged. "Nine. Ten. I can't remember."

"Of course, everyone has gotten older. You have as well. But look around." Liv scanned the crowd as she spoke. "There are also some new faces. Mingle. Get to know people."

"Pah. I don't mingle."

Liv's head dropped to her chest. It was going to be a long night.

"I'm thirsty," Anthony announced.

"I'll get you a drink." *And get myself a bus ticket to anywhere but here.*

"Remember, no sugar and no caffeine. That doctor has me on bread and water."

"Oh, you're exaggerating." She pulled a few of her business cards from her pocket. "Here. I could use some help starting a buzz about the restaurant."

"What is this?" He examined the cards.

"There's a coupon on the back."

He snorted. "Do I look like a salesman?"

The man was going to oppose her at every turn. "Yes, Papà, you do. You own the largest ranch in this town. I suspect you spent many years as a salesman and a negotiator."

"Someday you'll inherit that ranch, and you won't have to work a restaurant job."

Liv stared at her father for a moment, dismayed by his words, which said he hadn't listened to anything she'd said the last six times he brought this up. How hard was it to understand that the ranch was his dream and not hers?

Liv's eyes started to tear up and she fought the emotion. Why for once couldn't he understand and be happy for her?

"This isn't like my part-time job at the pizza place in Elk City, Papà. I *own* the restaurant."

"Fine. Fine," he muttered.

She closed her eyes for a half second, calming herself. This was her father, and she would respect him, no matter how unreasonable he was. Liv handed him the business cards.

"Please take the cards and support your daughter."

He released a tortured sigh and accepted them. "You're just like your mother."

"Thank you." Possibly the only thing they agreed on was her mother.

As Liv made her way to the beverage table, she passed a few familiar faces. Several smiled, a few eyed her curiously and one or two shot a dismissive glance.

She recognized the aged editor of the *Homestead Pass Daily Journal.* The man frowned, his bushy white brows meeting each other as he turned away from Liv's greeting.

Liv paused at the response and then worked to shake it off. Maybe he was hard of hearing, or maybe she was becoming paranoid about her reception tonight. She'd networked at dozens of events like this, promoting whatever restaurant she was consulting.

However, there was never an emotional tie-in or a history. She couldn't deny being nervous.

After all, her quick in-and-out visits to Homestead Pass had protected her from the fallout of her actions years ago. Until tonight.

Sam was well-loved by everyone in town. Of all the Morgan boys, he was the one who had cultivated a relationship with many of the townsfolk. He had the trifecta—brains, good looks and was a jock in high school. Everyone loved Sam.

Even she loved Sam.

Not enough to marry him.

She pushed away the thoughts.

Liv spotted one of her favorite teachers from high school and crossed the room to greet the woman.

"Hello, Mrs. Morrow. How nice to see you. I'd be honored if you'd stop by my restaurant when it opens." Liv smiled and handed the woman a business card. "Show this to your server for twenty percent off your meal."

The woman offered a noncommittal harrumph as she took the card and looked it over. "Does this mean you're planning to stick around this time?"

"I, um…" Liv sputtered, her heart racing at the downright rudeness.

"Maybe I'll see you at Olivia's restaurant, Mrs. Morrow," came a deep voice. Liv and Mrs. Morrow looked up to see that Sam had joined the conversation. "I recommend the tiramisu."

He offered a slow smile for the schoolteacher, like she was the only woman in the room. All this time, Liv thought Lucas was the family charmer.

Immediately, Mrs. Morrow's icy features thawed. She cocked her head and smiled back, completely under his spell. "I suppose, if it's good enough for you, Sam." Tucking the card in her pocket, she patted his arm before turning away.

Seriously? Liv stood in stunned silence at the transformation in the woman's countenance. "Thank you for that," she finally said. "I hoped I wouldn't end up in a fistfight at my first community event."

Sam laughed. "Whether you stick around or not, I'm not going to let the woman run roughshod over anyone."

"I'm sticking around, Sam." She looked up at him. "I have invested everything in sticking around."

"Is that right?" He stared at her with intensity.

"Yes." She looked away and searched for a change in topic. "I didn't expect to see you here."

"Many of my clients attend. Showing up is good for business." He glanced around the room. "For the record, Mrs. Morrow is the exception. I've heard nothing but excitement about your restaurant."

"Really? What about the shop?"

"Curiosity. Lots of curiosity."

She nodded, pleased his response. "I'll take that as a positive."

"Speaking of business, how did Lucas do?"

Liv perked at the question, eager to compliment Lucas for all the hard work he'd done. "Your brother is amazing. He completed everything on my list and a few more things."

"Good. Remember, Drew will be available all day on Saturday. After the painting is done, let him help you set up the shelving."

"Won't you be there?" Liv had gotten

used to Sam offering his thoughts on everything from the lighting to the displays. Though she didn't tell him that.

"No. I'm behind on my day job." Sam's eyes narrowed as he looked across the room. He began to back away. "I've got to go. Talk to you later."

Liv turned to see who he was looking at and nearly ran into a petite whirlwind. "Hi there," the woman said. "We haven't met. I'm Mindy Ellwood." The woman's large gold hoop earrings peeked out from beneath her long blond hair.

"Olivia Moretti. Nice to meet you."

Mindy waved a hand in the air. "I own the boutique across the street. Glitz & Glam. Cute, fashion-forward clothes and accessories." Her gaze moved from Liv's denim shirtdress with its casual double leather belt, to her red suede cowboy boots. "Nice boots. I should stock boots."

"Thanks. Boots are essential in this town. I have a collection. All red. I bought these at the Hitching Post. It's over on Edison Avenue."

"I haven't been in there—yet." She smiled. "So. You're Sam's ex, I hear."

Sam again. "What I am is the owner of Moretti's Farm-to-Table Bistro and The Inspired Kitchen."

A perplexed expression crossed Mindy's face. Then she laughed. "Yes. I know that. But you used to be engaged to Sam Morgan, right?"

"That was a very long time ago."

"So you don't have a problem with him dating other women?"

"Excuse me?" Liv blinked at the rapid-fire question.

Mindy leaned close, her hoops swaying back and forth. "We gals have to stick together. I'd never trespass on someone else's property."

"If you're asking my permission, you should know that Sam is my landlord. Nothing more."

Relief swept across the blonde's fair features. "I'm so glad," she breathed.

Liv stared at Mindy for a moment. She couldn't believe she'd come to a business meeting only to repeatedly run into

Sam Morgan groupies. It was complicated enough to be sharing a business with her ex. She wasn't going to run interference on his love life as well.

"Would you excuse me?" Liv asked. "I promised my father I'd bring him a drink."

"Sure. Nice talking to you."

"Ah, yes. You too, Mindy."

Liv's gaze circled the room, finally landing on her father near the buffet, chatting with Mrs. Pickett and several other women.

"The widows' club."

She turned around to find her aunt standing next to her. "What?"

"The widows' club. They invited me to join and rescinded the invitation when I mentioned that I'd never been married." Loretta shrugged. "Their loss."

Liv marveled at her aunt. "Here I am hoping to fit in and you're so laid-back about everything." She paused. "Maybe I'll never get married. I want to be you when I grow up, Zia."

"Rilassato," her aunt said. "That's Italian for laid-back. When you reach a cer-

tain age, you realize that it's better to be yourself than fit in."

She pointed a finger at Liv in a familiar gesture. "Your attitude, my dear niece, is not determined by whether you are married or single, divorced or widowed. Don't make the mistake of walking away from love because you think it will take something from who you are. Real love, like real friendship, only adds to who you are."

Liv stared at her aunt, nodding slowly. "You're right," she murmured.

"Of course I am."

The discussion gave Liv pause. Did she want more than the restaurant? She hadn't allowed herself to think about the possibility of marriage and a family while she fought for her career. Could it be time to consider the possibility of more in her future?

Loretta nodded across the room. "Don't look now, but it appears Mrs. Pickett is winning. Your father just brought her a cup of coffee."

"Oh, my goodness." Liv did a double take as Mrs. Pickett placed a hand on her father's arm and smiled. "Whoa. Did you see that move? She certainly works fast."

"Not really." Loretta smiled tenderly. "They've known each other for years. Maybe this is what your father needed. A little female attention. How would you feel about him dating?"

She had thought about her father and Mrs. Pickett when the bookstore owner stopped by the restaurant. But not seriously.

"I want him to be happy." Liv finally got the words out. "He's been alone since Mama died. That's over twenty years."

"Oh, he's happy, all right. Bringing him with you tonight was genius."

"It wasn't my idea. It was Mrs. Pickett's," Liv said. Then she laughed. "I guess Mrs. Pickett is a genius."

"Well, well, well," Loretta murmured. "You're right. Points for Mrs. Pickett."

Liv smiled and released a sigh. Her father was lonely. How was it she hadn't figured that out? Tonight, his dark eyes sparkled as they hadn't in years.

In that moment, she vowed to do whatever she could to keep that smile on his face.

"Seriously, Sam? We had to meet after dark on a Friday night to unload your stuff?"

Sam chuckled at the indignation in Liv's voice. "Did you have other plans? I'm doing this for your benefit. To maintain the integrity of our competition. None of your staff will be in the shop at this hour."

"While that's correct, this might be overkill." She paused and looked at him, her stance defensive. "And I could have had plans. You don't have to sound like it's out of the realm of possibility."

"I didn't say that. I'm sure a dozen guys have already asked if they can slay dragons for you."

"Not a dozen. Only half a dozen."

He eyed her, not certain if she was serious and annoyed about the prospect of Liv dating right in front of him.

"Look, I'm taking this competition very seriously," he said. "You have the advantage. You're available to hand sell your product. I'm going into this blind with no ability to sway the customer with my sales spiel."

"I'll be in the restaurant most of the time. I don't have time to hand sell either. The product has to sell itself to the tourists."

"Hey, ye of little faith, my products will do that."

She unlocked the back door of The Inspired Kitchen and turned on the lights before propping the door open.

"Can you pull down the shades?" he asked with a glance over his shoulder.

"Fine," she huffed.

Sam lowered the tailgate of his truck and grabbed two boxes. He stood in the hallway looking around when Liv returned.

"All done, 007."

"Thanks. Where do you want these?"

"The storage room. On the left side. I won't be setting up until the paint dries."

"I'll need to explain each item and the pricing."

She shot him an impatient look. "You already provided me with the most detailed inventory I've ever seen. I can read."

Sam frowned, reluctant to share that this was the first time his babies were going out in the world. Yeah, he was nervous about their reception. Not to mention the fact that the boxes represented a huge financial investment. The cherry used in many of the pieces was an expensive hardwood in limited supply.

"Okay. Then, I guess you'll text me if you have questions." He met her gaze. "Any questions."

"I'll do that," Liv said.

They worked together unloading boxes. It didn't escape his notice how many times in the last few weeks they'd managed to pull together as a team.

"How many more are there?" Liv asked.

"A few."

"That's a lot of inventory." She headed to the truck and reached for a carton marked Fragile.

Yeah, it was a lot. He'd been working on these for a couple of years now.

"Careful, that one's fragile."

"I may not have been clear. I can read." Liv assessed the box. "What's fragile about wood?"

"Wood with ceramic." Sam grabbed another box and followed her in, opting to change the subject. "Next Thursday is the big day, right?"

"Yes," she said. "I can't wait. It's been weeks of nonstop burning the candle at both ends."

"I hear you. When does the restaurant open?"

"The soft launch is Thursday as well. Since most of the town will be at the spring dance on Friday, the official grand opening is Saturday."

"Are you going to the dance?" he asked.

"I'm thinking about it." She eyed him warily. "Would that be a problem?"

"I'm not sure." Liv under normal circumstances was a distraction and a disturbance in his universe. Did he really need to expose himself to the woman he thought he was going to spend his life with all glammed up and dancing with other fellas?

Liv chuckled. "Are you serious? What does 'not sure' mean?"

"Just what I said."

"Come on. A clarification is in order."

"It would be nice if we both could attend and fly under the radar, but you never know. Small town." He shrugged. "Our showing up may end up as fodder for the week's gossip."

"You're unnecessarily concerned," Liv said. "The small business meeting went fine. Didn't it?"

Sam only grunted, hoping she was right. The last thing he wanted was to be the topic of conversation among his friends.

He put a box on the floor, tore through the tape and pulled out a white oak and American black walnut striped cutting board. There was no holding back a smile. The piece was beautiful.

"By the way, all the products have an additional packing slip with pricing. Redundancy is built in, so there won't be any inventory errors."

"Thanks for the vote of confidence," Liv

said. She reached out to run her hand over the board. "This really is a stunning piece."

"Thanks." Sam's smile widened at the praise. "All my products have the initials *SJ* burned into the wood as well."

"*SJ?*" She looked at him. "As in *Samuel Joseph.*"

"Well, yeah, but no one else is going to figure that out. My business entity is registered with the state as Homestead Pass Woodworking. Nobody is going to put that together either."

"I hope you're right."

"I am. No one will uncover who *SJ* is unless you tell them."

"What about your family?"

"My family thinks I'm still making birdhouses. They won't even notice." He recalled his conversation with Gramps when he'd found out Liv rented the space. The words hurt, more than he cared to admit.

"Have they seen these pieces?" Liv asked.

"No, but it doesn't matter. What's the Bible say about that? 'A prophet is not without honor, save in his own country, and in his own house.'" He shrugged. "The same applies to you."

"What do you mean?"

"Your father is another example. You're a well-known chef who has accomplished much and is still accomplishing much, and he doesn't recognize that."

She blushed at his words. "That's very nice of you to say. I didn't think you understood that."

"I understand more than you realize, Liv." He glanced at her and looked away, surprised they were having a real conversation for once.

"What about you? When did you start getting serious about woodworking?" She smiled. "I remember those birdhouses too."

"About the time you left, I started focusing in earnest." He raised a shoulder. "Turned out I have a knack for sorting out my frustrations by playing with wood."

She nodded. "Your father was a woodcrafter. I'm sure you inherited your talent from him."

"It was a hobby for him. Ranching was his real love."

Liv straightened the row of boxes on the floor and peeked up at him. "Do you want to be a creator full-time?"

"I don't want to make that decision just yet." Truth was, he was afraid. Afraid that he'd look foolish in front of his family, pretending his dream could be his future.

"What's holding you back?" Liv cocked her head and searched his face.

"I'm not sure. Maybe when I get my shop back, I'll be ready to decide."

"*Your* shop?" She shot him an exasperated look. "You might want to start thinking about Plan B."

Plan B. Right. Every day since she'd left had been Plan B. If Liv hadn't come back to town and swiped his store out from under him, how many years would it have taken him to step out in faith and give his woodworking a chance?

It seemed providential that she'd knocked him out of his complacency like a tornado, coming into town, refusing to let anything get in the way of her own dreams.

Maybe he should have been as demanding years ago. Followed her and told her how much he loved her. But that wasn't him.

He glanced around the shop. For all her annoying demands, he admired Liv. She never gave up. She was bossy and demanding and determined. Maybe he should take notes.

Liv pulled the last box in the pickup bed closer and stopped. "This one's too heavy for me. What's in it? Rocks?"

"Let me show you." Sam pulled out a pocketknife and carefully cut through the packing tape. He brought out a parcel covered in Bubble Wrap and unwrapped it, revealing glossy, inlaid-wood boxes with brass latches.

Liv took one out and opened it up to reveal a velvet-lined interior. The scent of cedar rose up to meet them both.

"A miniature hope chest," she said. "This is beautiful."

"That's right. I sell them for engagements, christenings and graduations. They hold mementos."

"And hopes."

He nodded. Yeah, that was right. She got it.

"This is such a unique idea. Any bride would love to have this."

Silence stretched between them. Liv raised her head.

"Why did you say yes, if you didn't want to marry me?" he whispered.

Her quick intake of breath turned to silence as she clasped her hands together.

The night seemed to grow still around them as they stood at the pickup's tailgate. Overhead a few bugs flew in and out of the halo of the streetlight.

He studied her for a moment, realizing he was ready to know the truth. All of it.

"I think it's time to tell me what was in that letter I burned. Don't you?"

Smile fading, she offered a slow nod.

"I left town in June, on the anniversary of my mother's death," Liv said softly. She met his gaze, the brown eyes imploring him to understand.

"All my life, the story of how my mother

gave up everything for my father and the ranch has been repeated as my guidance for the future. The closer I came to my own future, the one my father had plotted out for me, the more terrified I became."

Liv bowed her head for a moment, tapped her sandals against the pavement rhythmically and then stopped. Once again, she looked at him.

He fought the urge to make this easy for her. He'd waited too long; it was okay if she was uncomfortable for a few minutes.

"Sam, we never talked much about anything. First college, then culinary school. You were on the rodeo circuit. Then I started traveling for my job. We fell into a pattern, and it seemed there wasn't time for deep discussions."

"I don't buy that, Liv. I would have made time."

She opened and closed her hands, biting her lip and frowning before she looked him in the eye. "I couldn't talk to you about my father, because Morettis don't do that. Family business remains in the family.

Now, I realize that my silence was far worse than breaking the unspoken rules."

Once again, silence stretched between them.

Sam glanced at her. "You could have turned me down. Told me you didn't love me." He averted his gaze. Was he ready to see the truth in her eyes?

"I did love you, Sam." Her sigh filled the silence. "But I couldn't see beyond my fear of my dreams being snatched away."

Her words failed to reassure him. All the miles they'd traveled together, and she didn't know him at all.

"Can you ever forgive me?"

He considered the heartfelt apology and took a deep breath before looking square into the concerned brown eyes. "I forgave you a long time ago."

"Will we be able to find our way back to friends?" she asked.

"I don't know, Liv. I don't know."

Chapter Six

Liv sat up in bed and smiled. A lazy Sunday seemed too decadent to be true. She'd
attended the early service at church, come
home and fallen asleep on top of her duvet
in her Sunday clothes. Clearing the air
with Sam yesterday had given her peace
of mind. He didn't know if they could be
friends, but she still felt lighter somehow.
The soft ticking of her bedside clock said
it was nearly 1:00 p.m. Time for lunch.

She changed into cut-off jeans, a short-
sleeved T-shirt and flip-flops before she
washed her face and pulled her hair into a
sloppy topknot.

The scent of simmering tomato sauce,

with hints of basil and oregano, teased her as she made her way downstairs. Liv entered the kitchen and did a double take. It was her father, instead of her aunt, at the stove.

"Are you cooking, Papà?"

"I've been cooking since long before you or my baby sister picked up a spatula. No need to look so surprised."

Surprised? She was stunned. Her father used to cook all the time before he lost the love of his life. He hadn't been in the kitchen since.

"Pleasantly surprised is what I meant." Loretta usually made the Sunday meal after church. This turn of events had Liv smiling. That business meeting on Thursday certainly had put a kick in her father's step.

Liv moved closer to the massive professional stove. A pot of water boiled on one burner, and velvety tomato sauce simmered on another.

"You're making sauce?" The surprises continued. Sauce was a lengthy commitment. She couldn't remember the last time he'd made it from scratch.

"I made it yesterday while you were at work. Nonna's secret recipe."

"With meatballs, sausage and pepperoni?"

He nodded, a mischievous smile on his face. "You better believe it. Someday I will share the recipe with you."

When her father turned his head and began to wash a head of romaine lettuce, Liv pulled a spoon out of the drawer and snuck a spoonful of the rich, ruby-colored liquid. "Oh, my goodness, this is delicious. What's the occasion?"

"Sunday lunch." He swatted her hand. "Stay out of that."

Liv laughed and sniffed the air. There was more going on here than sauce, though she couldn't quite put her finger on the origin of the aroma. "What's in the oven?"

"Eggplant parmigiana." Her father's expression became serious. "What about that sermon today? Lots to think about, eh?"

"Philippians?" she asked, blinking at the random change of subject.

"Yes." He nodded. "'Reaching forth unto those things which are before.'"

"Sounds like you've given it some thought. What does that mean to you, Papà?"

"Perhaps it means I'm ready to start thinking about the future. A different future than I'd planned."

"I'm glad to hear you talking like that." She hoped that meant he was also ready to consider a future without her taking over the ranch.

"Are you?" He cocked his head and studied her.

"Of course. I want you to be happy."

"And I want my daughter to be happy."

"I *am* happy."

"You should get out more." He eyed her. "I'm going to the spring dance." He pushed his shoulders back and grinned.

Whoa! "I'm so proud of you, Papà. I bought tickets. Does that count?"

"You have to actually go."

"I recognize a pot-calling-the-kettle theme here." She turned. "I'm going to set the table."

"It's already set."

Liv entered the dining room, where a festive blue-and-yellow-print tablecloth and her father's favorite Mediterranean dinnerware adorned the table. The colorful ceramic plates in hues of red, blue and yellow were usually reserved for special occasions.

She counted the place settings. Five?

"Do we have guests coming?" she called.

"Can't get anything by you." Her father chuckled, the ever-present wheeze audible.

An uneasiness bubbled inside Liv. "Who's coming to dinner?"

"Eleanor."

She frowned. Was Mrs. Pickett's first name Eleanor? Or had he invited another woman to dinner?

"Eleanor Pickett?" she called out.

"That's the one."

Liv glanced back at the table. She counted the place settings one more time. It was still five. "And who else?"

The doorbell rang, startling Liv.

"My hands are full," her father called. "Please get the door."

"Papà, you didn't answer my question."
The doorbell sounded again.

"Get the door, Olivia. Don't leave our guests waiting."

Liv grumbled under her breath, her gaze on the extra place setting. An uneasy feeling began in her stomach, as she quickly moved past the living room to the entry hall and pulled open the door.

"Mrs. Pickett, how lovely to see you. Please, come in."

"Hello, dear." The woman beamed. "Please, call me Eleanor. Your father does."

Liv began to shut the door when Eleanor raised a finger. "You might want to wait. Someone else pulled in behind me."

"Oh, okay." Liv gestured behind her. "My father is in the kitchen, right down the hall."

"Down the hall." Eleanor nodded.

Liv stepped outside in time to see Sam strolling up the flagstone path, which was lined with blooming rose-pink azaleas. He moved toward the front door with flowers in his hand, and she hurried to meet him.

"Sam?" she whispered. "What are you doing here?"

He stopped, confusion on his face. "Your father didn't tell you I was coming."

A statement. Not a question.

"No, but..." Liv was at a loss for words. She hadn't seen him since their heart-to-heart on Friday night. Did he think she'd had a hand in orchestrating this get together?

"I can leave."

She waved a hand, ushering him toward the house. "No, please. Come in. You're very welcome. I'm just surprised."

"You and me both. I didn't know you'd be here."

"I live here."

"I know that, but your father made it sound like you wouldn't be here. I ran into him at the post office yesterday, and we chatted about his breeding program." Sam shrugged. "He asked me to stop by for pasta. And to see his bull." Sam looked at her, opened his mouth and then closed it, shaking his head.

Liv started laughing. "Bull, huh?"

"Okay, that would be funny, except I'm here, and I can't believe I fell for this. Are you sure you want me to stay?"

"Yes. Of course."

Liv glanced at the flowers, a massive bouquet of multicolored gerbera daisies, which happened to be her favorite. Sam was well aware of that detail.

"This is awkward."

Exactly what she was thinking.

He gestured with a hand toward the flowers. "They're for your aunt."

"That's very sweet of you."

"I'm a sweet guy. I guess you never noticed."

"Fair shot," Liv murmured. She deserved the remark. He was right. There was a lot about Sam she hadn't noticed. Self-involvement seemed to be her MO five years ago.

Liv found herself assessing Sam as though he was a stranger. He wore dark Wranglers and a blue dress shirt that brought out the vibrancy of his eyes. The dark hair grazed his collar, and his face held the shadow of stubble. The kind that made her want to lay her palm against his cheek.

Liv swallowed, appalled at her wayward thoughts. Then she blinked, remembering her hair and her clothes. She probably looked like a toddler with messy curls in a haphazard knot on top of her head.

Sam reached around her to open the door, and she hurried inside.

"My father's in the kitchen," Liv said quickly. "You know the way." She put on a smile. "Would you excuse me a moment?"

Liv took the stairway to the second floor two steps at a time and barreled into her bedroom. She brushed her unruly hair then pulled it back with a wide silver-and-turquoise clip, before changing into clean jeans. Loretta was waiting for her at the bottom of the stairs when Liv descended.

"Sam Morgan brought me flowers," her aunt said with a lift of a brow.

"I know," Liv returned.

"I can't recall the last time someone brought me flowers. What a lovely gesture…"

"That's Sam. Are you aware that we're

hosting a luncheon?" Liv asked. "Mrs. Pickett—I mean, Eleanor—is here as well."

Loretta nodded. "Anthony told me he was inviting her over. You were asleep, or I would have warned you." She paused. "I think it's great. Don't you?"

"Yes. A heads-up would have been nice. I had no idea Eleanor and Sam had been invited."

"I only found out when I came down to start cooking. Anthony told me he wanted to cook and to stay out of the kitchen. I thought it was a good sign. He's been acting very chipper since that meeting."

"Did you know that he's going to the spring dance?"

Loretta gasped. "No!"

"Yes. Things are moving quickly."

"Your father is quite the bulldog when he's made a decision."

"Don't I know it."

"Ready to go in?" Loretta asked.

Liv glanced toward the dining room and rubbed the back of her neck while trying to sort out what was going on. "I guess so."

"Why are you so tense?" Loretta asked.

"Sam didn't know I'd be here. It was awkward, and I hope I didn't make him feel unwelcome by my surprise."

"This isn't on you. Your father is making mischief. Another sign that he's feeling better. He hasn't pulled a stunt like this in years." Loretta laughed and sniffed the air. "Do you smell that?"

"Tomato sauce? Or maybe it's the basil in the eggplant."

"No. I smell drama. Your father loves drama." Loretta raised her brows. "Don't give him any."

"Why didn't we inherit the drama gene?" Liv asked.

"We got the ravishing-beauty gene instead."

The comment had Liv laughing again, her tension slipping away.

"Just remember. Your father is trying to stir up trouble. Do not give him what he wants."

Liv took a deep breath as she grabbed her aunt's arm. "Okay, I'm going to relax and pretend Sam Morgan is just another cowboy. No big deal. It's only supper, right?"

Loretta chuckled. "Oh, my dearest, I'll be praying for you."

Sam moved his knee and bumped Liv's. Again. "Sorry," he murmured.

He eyed Anthony at the head of the table, smiling benevolently at his kingdom. Loretta Moretti sat at the other end, with Mrs. Pickett across from Sam and Liv. As Sam recalled, the dining room table had an insert to expand the seating. Not today. Today the setup seemed purposely intimate.

Too intimate. So far, his knee had bumped Liv's half a dozen times. Each time she moved, the scent of her perfume drifted to him. The torture seemed endless.

He should have listened to his gut when he saw Liv standing on the flagstone path and made a quick exit. After their chat Friday night, he hadn't gotten much sleep thinking about her admission. He'd realized that it wasn't all on her. Shouldn't he have sensed there was a problem? Maybe he was too wrapped up in his own life to notice the red flags in their relationship back then.

"You're not eating, Sam," Anthony said.

Sam blinked. "Sorry. I was thinking." He picked up his fork.

"Thinking about Olivia?" Anthony's brows rose and his lips twitched.

"Yes, sir. I was thinking that she learned how to cook from the best. This is delicious."

Liv elbowed him and a meatball tumbled from his fork back to the plate.

"Yes, my daughter is a fine cook, Sam. I'm thrilled that she is home and ready to settle down." He offered Sam a wink.

Sam speared the little meatball again and shoved it in his mouth to avoid a response.

The room was silent for a moment, though Anthony seemed oblivious to the tension.

Loretta cleared her throat and picked up her water glass, while Eleanor's gaze darted from Anthony to Liv.

"Sam is correct. That was delicious," Eleanor finally said.

"Thank you." Anthony clasped his hands together, his eyes sparkling. "I love having my family around the table."

"Sam, would you please help me clear the table?" Liv pushed back her chair, again bumping his knee as she stood up.

"Wha—" The request took him by surprise, but he quickly recovered and got to his feet. "Yeah, sure."

Loretta started to rise. "I'll help."

"Sit, Zia. Sam will help." Liv's steely gaze had Loretta raising a hand and her brows.

"Start the espresso, will you?" Anthony asked.

"Yes, Papà." She offered her father a stiff tight-jawed smile that Sam recognized. Liv was not happy.

He picked up plates and followed her into the kitchen through the swinging door, barely keeping up.

"Where do you want these?" Sam glanced around the spacious kitchen, as familiar to him as his own.

Liv swung around sharply. "I'll take them."

"Just tell me where to put them."

"The counter is fine." Clearly agitated, Liv pulled the large espresso maker from the cupboard and filled it with water and grounds before placing it on the stove and lighting the burner.

"My father," she muttered.

"There's no point getting upset. It's only lunch." He rubbed a hand over his face.

"Only lunch," she scoffed.

"Now that I see what's going on, I should probably tell you the rest of the story."

Liv turned from the stove. Dark, stormy eyes pinned him. "What story?"

"I did run into your father at the post office, and he did talk to me about the breeding program. But that's not all he said."

Her indrawn breath filled the silence. "You lied to me?"

"I omitted information. Your father told me that he thought of me like a son." He grimaced, looked at her and then away. "I figured you didn't want to hear that line again."

Liv groaned. "The son he never had."

"He said he'd like to break bread with me one more time before he met the good Lord. Then he invited me to lunch today. The inference was that you would not be present." Sam lifted his hands. "What would you have done?"

"Why, that wily conniver." She raised her head to meet Sam's gaze. "So I'm right. This was a setup, wasn't it?"

"What's the harm? We shared a delicious meal, and besides a few awkward knee bumps, neither of us were irreparably damaged." Sam smiled, hoping to lighten things. "Right?"

Pink color flushed Liv's face at his words. "That's not the point, Sam. He manipulated both of us."

"Olivia, please bring the gelato," her father called.

"Yes. Papà." Liv uttered another groan before pointing to the cupboard above the dishwasher. "Gelato bowls are in there."

"I remember." Yeah, all he did was remember. He'd been in this kitchen so many times he'd lost count. He had always tried to be available when Liv was home from one of her culinary training jobs.

After grabbing a container from the freezer, Liv yanked open the kitchen drawer, sending the utensils clattering. Then she whirled around, her fingers tightly clutching a metal scoop.

Sam jumped back. "Easy there."

"Sorry," she murmured.

For minutes, they worked like a team, serving up dessert. Sam placed five crystal bowls on the counter, and Liv filled each with a scoop of pale lemon gelato and a sprig of mint. Then she added them to a tray with dessert spoons. Sam reached for the tray at the same time she did, and their fingers tangled. Liv pulled away quickly.

"I've got this," he said.

"Fine. I'll bring in the coffee. That will give me a moment to calm down."

Sam pushed open the door and put on a smile. The entire situation was laughable. There was one thing he could say about the Morgans. They were boring compared to the spirited Moretti family.

Small talk began to wan after coffee

and dessert, and as it did, Anthony gazed fondly upon his only child.

"Olivia, why don't you show Sam the new bull?"

She crossed her arms. "I don't think Sam wants to see the bull."

Sam kicked her leg under the table. Liv jerked and then glared at him.

"Sure I would." He stood, working to hide a laugh. Liv was downright adorable when she was dressed in all that indignation.

"All right, then," she muttered, pushing back her chair. "Bull, it is."

Sam followed her out of the house and down the walk, his long legs barely keeping up with her. Story of his life. Liv running away.

He and Drew were at the tux fitting when Gramps called to say Liv had dropped by and left a manila envelope for him. His grandfather said Liv looked like she'd been crying. He was sure something was wrong.

Yeah, something was wrong. There was a letter and his ring tucked inside the envelope.

Could he have changed the outcome if he'd been home? That question had haunted him for a long time.

The stables sat a distance from the house. Liv kept moving, her red boots kicking up a cloud of dust as she went. At her current pace, she would reach them in about five minutes, no doubt besting her high school track record.

"Slow down," he called. "I'm not as young as I used to be."

Liv slowed her pace a fraction. "What would you like to see that you haven't seen?"

"What's changed around here? Bowie Stewart still managing the ranch?"

"Yes." She stopped and turned, waiting for him as though the anger fueling her had run dry. "Do you really want to see the bull?"

Sam chuckled. "We've got our share on the Lazy M."

"Come on, then," she said. "I'll show you my father's other pride and joy. Though he can't ride him at the moment."

"Why can't he ride?" Sam asked as he matched his pace to hers.

She sighed. "Health issues. Cardiac and pulmonary along with a bad hip."

Sam grimaced.

"His cardiologist says he has carotid artery stenosis. He's on medication, but he's not a candidate for an endarterectomy right now."

"Meaning?"

"His carotid artery is blocked with plaque." Bleakness clouded her eyes as she looked at him. "He's pretty much a walking time bomb. If he doesn't have the procedure it's likely he'll have a stroke."

Sam stiffened at the words. Anthony was at least twenty years younger than Gramps. He'd be devastated if his grandfather was ill. "Can't they fix that?"

"Normally, yes. But the doctor won't risk the procedure until he's in better pulmonary health. He's recovering from a bout of pneumonia. Right now, the horses, the cattle, the hay. Exertion. Everything contributes to his already diminished lung capacity, which then impacts his heart."

"Wow, that's tough."

"My father has always thought he was immortal, refusing to go to the doctor for regular checkups. To his credit, he's a much better patient than he was years ago, and he's given up most of his unhealthy vices. Being unable to manage his ranch as he'd like has been a wake-up call."

After a moment, he said, "That's why you moved home."

"Yes."

"It's also why you aren't opening your dream restaurant in New York or Denver."

She nodded, her gaze fixed on the stables ahead.

"I'm sorry, Liv. I was kind of a jerk about it when I asked, wasn't I?"

"Yes."

Sam laughed. He could always count on Liv to be honest. Except the one time she wasn't. When he asked her to marry him.

He reached for the wrought iron, stable-door handle and moved the door, sliding it along a track, then allowed her to enter first.

Liv strode down the rubber pavers of the

stable aisle and stopped at a stall on the right. "Meet Mr. Dean Martin."

"Seriously?" Sam couldn't help but grin as he assessed the dappled bay with a black mane and tail.

"Yep. This is Dino." The horse nickered when Liv ran a loving hand over his mane.

"Beautiful animal."

Liv faced him. "What do you think about taking a ride?" she asked almost shyly.

They hadn't ridden together in a very long time. Riding with Liv was about yesterday. For a moment, he hesitated. Did he really want to think further about the past today?

Before he could refuse, his big mouth opened and words tumbled out. "Yeah, sure. Why not?"

A shimmer of excitement lit her eyes. "Take that roan in the next stall. He's one of my favorites." Liv pointed. "Tack room is—"

"I know where the tack is." He was starting to sound like a broken record.

Liv worked quickly, tossing a saddle blanket on the back of a chestnut mare with white socks and smoothing the covering with care. Like him, Liv had been riding since she was a child, and it showed. Her movements were efficient and graceful.

She reached for the saddle and was astride well before he was, her gloved hand on the horn. Maybe this was a competition as well.

Sam rolled up the sleeves of his shirt before he swung into the saddle and nodded to indicate he was ready. Exiting the stables, he glanced at the blue sky. A few clouds provided cover from the sun. Mid-May, and already the temperatures inched toward eighty. He hadn't expected to be on a horse, or he would have brought his hat.

A few minutes down the path, Liv turned in her saddle, then straightened again. "Just checking. I don't want to lose you."

"You're not going to lose me." The irony of the words didn't escape him.

"How often do you ride?" she asked.

"Not as much as I used to. What about you?"

"As often as I can," Liv returned.

Sam's brows raised. So, the red cowboy

boots weren't for show. "The lure of your ranching roots?"

"I suppose so. Like it or not, I'll always be a cowgirl at heart."

As the trail forked, Liv pointed to the right. "There's a man-made pond that was added last year up ahead about a quarter of a mile. Let's stop there."

Sam nodded.

They rode in silence for a while before coming to a semicircle of tall junipers sheltering a large pond.

Sam dismounted and hung the reins on the branches of a nearby tree. Liv followed suit.

"Pretty spot." He walked to the bank and stared into water so clear that he could see pollywogs wiggling at the bottom.

"Natural well feed into the pond?" he asked.

"Yes. A landscaper came in to level out the bank and created a rain culvert to prevent flooding. He did the aqua-scaping as well."

She stood next to him and ran a hand slowly over the top of a wall of knee-high horsetail reed. The grass swayed and then straightened like dutiful soldiers.

In the distance, Angus cattle grazed in a pasture of spring grass, unbothered by the heat and humidity.

"How many head of cattle is your father running these days?" Sam asked.

"I don't even know, though I heard him talking with Bowie, and I know they cut way back when my father got sick last winter. They've also had a hard time keeping help."

Sam nodded. "It's a tough life. My brothers will stay with the land forever. I'm the odd one. I enjoyed the ranch growing up. Now I want something more."

"Like what?"

"That's the question I keep asking myself." He gave a soft chuckle.

If he was honest, he'd admit that the whole competition with Liv was mostly bravado. He wasn't certain how his crafts would sell. Would they be a means to a future? Or was he fooling himself? Maybe he was destined to be a cowboy bean counter for the rest of his life.

They continued talking though Sam noticed that they both skirted around discussion of the past.

Still, he couldn't help but notice they were talking like they used to, in the days before her job and his rodeoing kept them apart.

Sam watched Liv for a moment, until she turned her head and smiled. "What?" she asked.

"Do you think if we'd spent more time talking like this years ago, things might have ended up different between us?"

"I don't know," she murmured. The words almost sounded wistful.

From the corner of his eye, he noticed Liv check her watch.

"Someplace you have to be?"

"My sous-chef is arriving tonight. It's Robyn. You remember her from college? She's driving from Oklahoma City, and she'll stay at the cottage. I've got plenty of time." She looked at him. "She has a job in Boston that she postponed so she could help me. It's a huge favor and I'm very appreciative."

"That's a great friend."

"She is."

An awkward silence stretched, and he knew she was thinking the same thing he was. He and Liv used to be the best of friends too.

"Should we head back?" Sam asked.

"Yes." Liv sighed. "I'm going to have to deal with my father."

"Maybe you could let it go. His heart is in the right place. You're fortunate to have someone who cares so much."

She nodded, looking out across the pond. "That I am fortunate is a given. However, it's not without its challenges."

"What's going to happen to the ranch?"

"That's a good question. I don't know."

"Isn't there a compromise somewhere?"

She turned toward him. "You think I should take over?"

"Not necessarily, but I do think that maybe you've been so opposed to the idea for so long that you haven't stopped to think about possibilities." He looked at her. "You compromised with your restaurant location. Life is all about compromises."

"I know you're right, but that's a lot of reality to handle at one time."

"Yeah, it is." Sam reached for the reins and mounted his horse. He looked over at her. Her dark curls were tangled, and her eyes sparkled with life. He'd missed times like this with Liv.

"This was nice." He wanted to say more but didn't.

"Like old times." Liv looked at him. "Is that what you were going to say?"

Sam shook his head. "No, not like old times. You and I can't go back, but I'm starting to think maybe we can go forward."

Something he couldn't decipher flickered in her dark eyes.

"We have too much history to walk away from our friendship, Liv. Let's work on being friends again."

"That's all I want, Sam. The chance to be friends again."

He gave the horse a nudge, praying he

hadn't made a mistake. Could he keep his heart and his head from talking to each other about the wisdom of such a decision? He sure hoped so.

hadn't made a mistake. Could he keep his
heart and his head from talking to each
other about the wisdom of such a decision?
He sure hoped so.

Chapter Seven

L iv stared out the rain-dappled windows
of The Inspired Kitchen. The television
meteorologist had promised May would
live up to its reputation as the wettest
month of the year.

So far, he'd been right. It was Friday, and
the rain had been nonstop since Thursday.
She prayed Saturday's Memorial Day pa-
rade didn't get rained out.

The good news was that after four
twelve-hour days in the kitchen with the
new team, the soft launch of the restaurant yesterday had been a success. Loretta
brought along her book club friends and
staff had invited family members to fill the
restaurant for their first service.

Her father had declined the invitation, but with Eleanor's urging, promised to visit once the restaurant was officially open. Disappointment was Liv's first response. She longed to show him what she'd built.

Then she realized she would have been a nervous wreck with her father around yesterday.

He would have noticed, as Loretta did, that the tomato sauce had a hint too much salt. However, Loretta's delivery of the information was much more generous than her father's would have been.

The servers only broke one plate. The unfortunate collision outside the kitchen door prompted Liv to pick up mirrors at the hardware store to assist with traffic flow.

All in all, they were on solid ground, so today, Liv left Robyn in charge of tomorrow's prep while she concentrated on the home goods shop.

The front door chimes sounded, and Liv and her store manager, Jane Smith, looked up. The mail carrier came in with a box and a stack of mail, smiling despite the weather. "Afternoon, ladies," she said. "I had to drop off this box, so I thought I'd also bring your mail. Save you a trip to the post office."

"That was really nice of you," Liv said.

"No problem," the carrier returned with a smile.

No problem, but it was a big deal. Personal kindness meant something. It was something Liv had forgotten about until she'd returned to Homestead Pass. She had many wonderful experiences in San Francisco, Boston, New York and the dozens of other cities she had called home for the length of a contracted consultation. But Homestead Pass was special.

Jane appeared at her side and peeked at the box. "Anything fun?"

"Brochures to hand out to customers."

"Oh." The older woman nodded. "I think I'll dust."

There was no dust, but Liv wasn't about to discourage her. Things were slow today, but she expected them to pick up on Saturday, the official start of the three-day weekend.

Ten minutes later, the chimes sounded again, and Liv looked up from her mail to see Mindy Ellwood bounce into the store with a grin. She closed her pink umbrella and placed it in the stand Liv had situated next to the front door.

"Hi, there. I had a few minutes, so I thought I'd check out your store and bring you your mail. Love the name of the shop, by the way."

"Thanks." Liv frowned. "My mail was just delivered."

"Mine as well." Mindy pulled two letters from the pocket of her clear polka-dot rain slicker. "They were stuck inside my bridal magazines."

"I didn't realize you were getting married." Apparently, Drew Morgan's intel on the bubbly shopkeeper was off.

"Oh, I'm not. I like to be prepared." She winked.

"Oh! Good plan."

Mindy walked around the shop, her fingers lingering over some of Sam's pieces. "I don't suppose you're interested in a little professional courtesy between businesses. Trading products."

"I could do that, except the woodcrafts in the shop aren't mine."

"No?" She wandered over to a display of coasters made with multiple cuts of wood to create a stripe pattern. "These are beautiful. The craftsmanship is amazing."

Mindy was examining the small cutting boards now.

"Who's the craftsman?" the blonde asked.

"Local artisan. He wants to keep a low profile, and I respect that."

"Do you know what kind of wood this is?"

Liv walked up, flipped the tag over. "Cherry and maple."

"Are there any more? These would make great Christmas presents. But there are only six. I'd need a dozen."

"I can hold these behind the counter and special order six more."

"Yes. Let's do that." Mindy picked up the cutting boards and handed them to Liv before moving on to the charcuterie boards.

She raised her brows as she examined one. "A bit pricey, isn't it?"

"It's olive wood and comes with four stainless steel utensils. I know for a fact that boards like this go for double at specialty stores in Oklahoma City and Tulsa." Liv leaned closer and lowered her voice. "This is the last one."

"I'll take it."

Liv kept a straight face as she carried the board to the counter. In light of the competition between herself and Sam, she probably should have steered Mindy to the home goods on the other side of the store, instead of the wood products. But she could not in good faith do that.

Sam's products were exceptional.

"I've seen Sam Morgan in here a few times," Mindy said. She admired her nails, then peeked at Liv.

"Didn't we already discuss this? He owns the building. I'm sure you saw him completing repairs." Liv clipped off the price tag and inspected the piece, then carefully documented the purchase on the inventory sheet for Sam's merchandise.

"I wonder if you can help me." Mindy slid her credit card across the counter but didn't release it.

Liv looked at her and then at the card. Mindy moved her fingers.

"Help you? Are you asking about the care of the board? The care guide is on the back of the tag. If you have any other problems, I can speak to the artist."

Mindy tapped her long nails on the counter and sighed. "No. I'm asking about Sam."

"Sam?"

"Yes. He's sort of tough to get a handle on, isn't he?"

"Is he?" She glanced at Mindy. "What makes you say that?"

"He bought me coffee, which I took as an encouraging sign. And now? I haven't seen a glimpse of the man. It's like he's avoiding me." Her voice was laced with frustration.

"Men." Liv tore off a large sheet of brown wrapping paper with force. "Isn't that just the way it works? They're only interested when you aren't."

"Are you sure you two aren't an item?" Mindy gestured with her hands.

"Why do you keep asking that?"

"Mrs. Pickett seems to think that you are."

Liv sighed. "Mrs. Pickett also thinks Elvis and Priscilla will reunite."

Mindy's eyes rounded.

"I rest my case."

The front door opened, its chimes interrupting the conversation. Liv's friend Robyn walked in, working to close her umbrella. The redhead ran a hand through her pixie cut, which was tousled by the wind.

"Mindy, will you excuse me?" Liv turned to the store manager. "Mrs. Smith will complete your purchase for you."

"Of course." Jane stepped up to the counter.

"Are you going to the dance?" Mindy called.

Liv had planned to skip the event until Mindy's interrogation.

"Absolutely." The word was out there before she could consider the consequences.

Liv sighed. Maybe, like her father, she *was* drawn to drama.

"Let's go." Liv pulled Robyn out the door. "How did you know I needed rescuing?"

Robyn opened the umbrella and Liv ducked beneath it as they started down the street.

"Are you kidding? It was either save you or call 9-1-1. I was window shopping when I saw you. You looked like a meme of a deer in the headlights."

"The woman is relentless. She wants dirt on Sam."

"Is there any dirt?"

"The man loves God, his family and his country. The only dirt on Sam Morgan is the red clay on his boots."

Robyn stepped around a puddle on the sidewalk. "And you're sure you don't want him?"

"Of course I want him. As a friend. He's the kind of friend who will always have your back."

Liv frowned as she said the words, a knot

forming in her stomach. So why did she find Mindy's interest in Sam so annoying?

"He stopped by looking for you this morning."

"Sam stopped by the restaurant?"

"Yes. I gave him a couple of tarts and sent him on his way."

"What did he want?"

"It doesn't matter. I told him you had plans, and I didn't know when you'd be available." Robyn pointed a finger. "A woman should never be too available."

Liv laughed. "What are you talking about?"

"Sam." Robyn smiled. "He's even more attractive than he was when we were in college."

"He's aged well. I'm sure he did that on purpose to irritate me."

Robyn laughed. "It's a good thing I'm already spoken for, or I might be tempted to trample over the private property signs into your territory."

Liv straightened. "It's not my territory. Besides, I don't have time for anything but the restaurant for at least a year. Then I can think about having a life."

Though it certainly wouldn't be Sam Morgan she'd be thinking about. She needed a man who didn't expect her to be home for dinner every night. Someone who understood that running a business meant long and unpredictable hours. A guy who got it if she had to fly out of town at the last minute for a job.

Not that she'd have to do that anymore, but it was the principle of the thing.

"Right." Robyn glanced around. "You've done a great job with both the restaurant and your shop, Liv. I know they're both going to be successful."

"Thank you." Liv smiled. The words meant so much. After years of making everyone else's dreams come true, it was finally her turn.

"Where are we going?" Robyn asked when Liv guided her to the crosswalk.

"I want to peek into Glitz & Glam, and then I thought we'd get coffee. There's a lovely coffee shop around the corner from the bookstore."

"You have your own espresso machine at the restaurant."

"Yes, but it's always nicer when someone else makes coffee for me. Besides, they have divine biscotti. Homemade."

"Ooh! Walk faster."

They crossed the street and stopped outside Mindy's shop. "That's a pretty dress." Liv pointed to a red sheath on the mannequin in the window.

"It is. Are you going to that dance tonight?" Robyn asked.

"Yes. Someone made up my mind for me."

"That woman in your shop?"

"How did you know? And by the way, she happens to own this boutique." Liv glanced at Robyn.

"The smoke coming out of your ears was my first clue. I haven't seen you so irritated in a long time. Maybe since that chef in Kansas City kept calling you baby doll." Robyn let out a laugh. "Too bad I can't go tonight."

"I'm sorry as well." Liv smiled. "Tell your darling fiancé I said hello."

"I will." Robyn looked up and down the street. "Homestead Pass is a postcard town. So pretty. But what's the draw? I mean, you said tourism is big economics here."

She nodded. "Route 66. We're on the historic route, and it leads straight to Elk City and the Route 66 Museum. More importantly, you have to go through Homestead Pass to get to Braum's Ice Cream. That's a lot of traffic on the way to get a cherry limeade."

Liv glanced around, seeing the town from her friend's eyes. Despite that her plans had changed, her hometown wasn't a bad location to set up shop.

"You're very fortunate to live here," Robyn said. "Are you settling here for good?"

"I'm home for good, unless the restaurant fails. Seventeen percent of them fail in their first year. I just have to be in that eighty-three percent."

"I think you've got this." They ducked beneath the canopy of the Book Nook and Robyn peeked in. "I'll have to find time to stop in here."

"It's a fun little bookstore." Liv turned her head and looked inside the big bay window. She gasped. "Am I seeing things? Is that my father?"

"It certainly is." Robyn chuckled. "I'm not a body language expert, but I think he's flirting with that pretty woman with the silver-blond hair."

"Mrs. Pickett." She tugged on Robyn's arm. "Let's go. I don't want him to see me."

"Are you okay?"

"I'm fine. I knew he and Eleanor were…" Liv waved a hand in the air. "What do you call it when your seventy-year-old widowed father's face lights up when a particular woman walks into the room?"

Robyn started laughing. "Love. I call it love, my friend."

"Love? Do you think that's good for his heart condition?"

"Yes, Liv. Love is medicine for the soul."

Sam glanced around the school gymnasium, the only space in town large enough for the spring dance. He smiled. Despite the stars hanging from the ceiling and the twinkling lights, it still looked like the gym to him.

Many good memories had been created in this place. Varsity basketball. Senior prom. Commencement.

His senior year was when his and Liv's relationship began a transformation that kept them connected through college. Even when Liv traveled all over the country for her job, they managed to keep their relationship afloat.

Every now and again, he tried to figure out what had gone wrong, and then gave up. Thinking about Liv's defection started a dull ache in his head and left him confused. Her admission a week ago had only left him with more questions. He'd been focused on the rodeo and the ranch, not on Liv. More and more he realized that he was somewhat culpable as well.

The DJ had already set up on the stage and a soft country ballad warmed up the crowd of people circling the edges of the dance floor but not ready to commit.

Something made him turn toward the

entrance door, and when he did, he spotted Liv. Her hair was loose, touching her shoulders, and it moved when she turned her head to look around the room. Just the sight of her lifted his spirits. He hadn't seen her since Sunday at her father's house. Was it possible he missed her?

Sam wasn't going to analyze anything tonight. He would never have thought that he and Liv could return to the place they'd started from so many years ago. Friends.

They were moving in that direction, and he was glad. There was no point taking it apart and trying to figure it out. He'd roll with the situation for now.

Her face lit up when she saw him, and she crossed the room quickly. The rose-colored dress she wore floated around her legs as she walked. He noted she'd abandoned her boots for black strappy heels. He'd never seen a woman as beautiful as Liv. Lovely inside and out.

A few other fellas noticed her entrance as well, and he shot them warning looks.

"Why are you frowning?" she asked.

"Was I? No reason." He smiled. "Nice dress."

"Thank you." She blushed at his words. "Is your family here?"

"Gramps is here somewhere. He'd never miss free food."

"And your brothers?"

"Drew's family has that bug that's going around. Lucas has a big rodeo this weekend, and as for Trevor, well, he's not into anything that includes being social."

She nodded grimly. Liv was still in town when Trevor had lost his wife. It was understood that they didn't discuss his brother's woes.

"Looks like Anthony and Eleanor are getting along nicely," Sam noted.

Liv followed his gaze to the punch bowl, where her father was deep in conversation with Eleanor Pickett. Deep, as in they only had eyes for each other and hadn't noticed there was anyone else in the room.

"Getting along nicely? They've been inseparable since that business meeting. I don't get it."

Sam laughed. "Love at second sight, Liv."

"I guess. I only hope she doesn't break his heart."

He opened his mouth to comment and decided against pointing out the irony of her concerns.

"So, how'd it go with opening day at the shop?" he asked.

"Excellent. The store manager I hired is very efficient. Her name is Jane Smith. A retired librarian who lives in Elk City. I'll check in daily and do a bank run, but the store is off to a great start."

"Jane Smith." He rubbed his chin. "Sounds like a missing person report."

Liv looked at him, horrified. "Stop that. She has excellent references."

"If you say so. The important thing here is, have I sold out yet?"

She smiled. "I checked in with Jane before I left the house. You had quite a few sales, and I have a special order for the small cutting boards."

"I'm not taking special orders."

"Yes, you are. It's good for business."

"I'd rather not." Warning bells went off in his head. When would he find time for special orders?

"Fine," Liv said with a shrug. "Fill this order and I'll try not to make any further promises to customers hungry for your artistry."

"I'd appreciate that. I'm glad sales are off to a good start. Six weeks will be here before I know it." And he couldn't wait. He might have bitten off more than he could handle. Eventually, he'd have to decide if he was a rancher, an accountant or a woodcrafter.

"About that——"

Sam raised a hand. "We have a deal, Liv." No matter how amazing she looked tonight, he had to stay focused. A long-term partnership with his former fiancée was like riding a bull. It wasn't a matter of *if* he would get hurt, only when.

"I agreed under duress," Liv said. "All I'm saying is, maybe we should revisit the terms of this bargain. Do we really need it? I say we terminate the agreement."

"No. Absolutely not."

"Why not? You and I have been working together for over a month now. Everything has been running smoothly. I've stayed out of your way. So what's the problem?"

"A deal is a deal." He wouldn't pass up the chance to win back the space before her lease was up.

"You're being unreasonable," she said softly. "However, I didn't come here to argue. We can revisit the topic another time."

Not likely.

Silence stretched for a moment and then she looked at him. "Why did you stop at the restaurant this morning?"

"I, ah… I couldn't remember if I set the carbon monoxide alarms." *Liar.*

"You did. I saw you. They'd be going off if there was a problem. Wouldn't they?"

"You're right." Sam nodded since he couldn't exactly tell her that he had stopped by because he needed an excuse to see her. "Oh, and by the way, I'll be in Sacramento most of next week."

"You will?"

"Yeah, I'm taking Drew's place at an ag

and ranch symposium. He doesn't like to travel and leave Sadie with the babies. If you have any problems with the building, call Gramps. He'll find someone to handle the issue."

"There won't be any problems."

He paused, sensing something in her tone. "What?" he asked.

"Nothing. Have a great trip." She glanced around the room, not meeting his gaze.

A great trip? Not likely. He hadn't wanted to go to Vegas, and he didn't want to go to California. But Trevor couldn't very well leave the spread. Until Lucas settled down, traveling for ranch business was in Sam's future.

Sam looked across the crowd and saw a familiar perky blonde. He adjusted the collar of his tie, then sidestepped to get out of her line of sight. She kept looking, an excited smile on her face. He continued to shuffle back and forth from the left to the right.

"What's wrong with you?" Liv asked, looking him up and down. "You keep moving like your shoes are too tight."

"Me? Nothing."

"If it's nothing, then why do you keep looking around?" Liv asked.

"I'm trying to avoid someone, okay? It's not a big deal."

"Who?"

"I'd rather not say."

Liv turned, her gaze scanning the gym. She scoffed. "Mindy Ellwood."

"How did you know that?"

"I'm intuitive." She assessed him. "Why are you avoiding her?"

Sam ran a hand over his jaw. This was going to be downright humiliating.

"Sam?"

"If you want the truth, she had a few tax questions, so I bought her a cup of joe at the coffee shop. Turns out it really wasn't about business or even joe. It was about Sam."

"I'm not following."

"She thinks we're dating because I bought her a four-dollar cup of coffee." He grimaced and released a breath through his teeth. "I cannot believe I got myself into this fix. I'm old enough to know better."

To her credit, Liv didn't laugh, though her eyes were suspiciously bright.

She cocked her head and looked him up and down. "Why don't you simply tell her?"

"I thought I did already. Have you got any bright ideas?"

Liv hesitated. "You'll have to be firmer."

"You know, it was easy when I was younger. I could say I already have a girlfriend. You."

Her eyes popped at the admission, and she sputtered, as though searching for a response. "I... I'm sure she'll understand if you explain."

Explain what? That he was still hung up on his ex and denying it on a daily basis?

"I'm not big into hurting people's feelings," he finally said.

"Well, you have to tell her."

"Not today."

The music started, and Sam searched for the exits as Mindy began to weave her way across the room toward him with the determination of a bull aiming to lose a rider.

He turned to Liv. "Let's dance."

"What?" Her eyes rounded.

"Dance. Let's dance." He took her hand and pulled her to the dance floor. Minutes later, he dared to glance around the room. Mindy stood at the buffet, talking to Gramps, eyeing him. She wasn't happy.

Well, neither was he. Too late, he realized that the song was a slow number. He was dancing to a slow, romantic ballad with the woman he used to be in love with.

Sam cocked his head, listening as the music from the DJ's speakers blared.

He knew this song. Knew it well. An oldie-but-goodie. It used to be their song. Maybe Liv wouldn't notice. Sam peeked at her.

Liv began to hum softly. *She's noticed.*

They moved in sync. Effortlessly. It had always been that way. Her hand was soft in his, and each time they turned, the scent of vanilla and coconut destroyed his good intentions a little more.

"Remember this song?" he asked.

"I do," she murmured. "Homecoming dance, my senior year and you came back from college to take me."

216 The Cowboy Bargain

"We had some good times, didn't we?" Sam asked.

"Yes, we did." Her gaze met his, and her brown eyes were soft and warm. "Am I your decoy dance partner?"

"You could say that. Or you could say we're two old friends sharing a dance."

"Tell that to your grandfather and my father. They're looking at us like it's the opening day of fishing season." She nodded to the right where Gus and Anthony grinned and nodded with clear approval. And he couldn't help but notice that Mindy now danced with a fella he recognized from the hardware store—that was good. Maybe she had heard him.

As they circled the floor Sam was only too aware of the curious glances, the frowns and the smiles. Liv glanced around and noticed as well. She became pensive. "You aren't concerned people will think that you and I are...you know."

"You've asked me that before." He paused, considering the wisdom of honesty. "I used to think that was a problem, way back when that tornado hit. I've slept since then, and maybe I've had a little common sense kick in."

"What's that supposed to mean?"

"It means we share a past. As long as I don't get myself tangled up in your future, things will be just fine."

"You make it sound like I'm trouble."

Sam looked down at her upturned face. The wide brown eyes asked a question he didn't dare answer. His gaze strayed to her mouth, and he glanced away.

"Liv. You are trouble."

Chapter Eight

Liv sprinkled the prep table with flour and turned out the rough, sticky dough as lightning flickered through the windows of the empty restaurant. Dusting her hands with flour, she methodically shaped the mixture into a ball. A clap of thunder reverberated, and her hands paused for a moment and then continued working the dough, pushing it away, folding it over and giving it a quarter turn.

Rain tapped on the window, begging for her attention. She ignored the sound, preferring instead to focus on the product on the prep table.

Another day of rain in western Oklahoma, she mused.

It wasn't raining in Sacramento. She'd checked the weather forecast this morning. Sunny and warm. Low humidity.

The irony hadn't escaped her. Sam was traveling for his job, and she was in Homestead Pass testing bread recipes. She used to be the one traveling while he was at home. During those years, they barely had time for hello before she was off to another job.

Yes, she had made many assumptions about who Sam Morgan had become and what he wanted. He was shooting holes in all her preconceived notions.

Liv inhaled deeply as the wind blew into the room. Despite the rain, she had opened a window a few inches, allowing the fresh loamy fragrance of outdoors to mingle with the yeasty kitchen scents.

A glance at her phone, propped on the shelf overhead, reminded her of the late hour. Maybe she'd stick the dough in the fridge and head home. Tomorrow was Friday, and the reservations list indicated that it would be a busy night.

Like the soft launch, the opening of the restaurant had been nearly perfect. She had been hustling all week.

But, busy was good. It left no time to think about the road that had brought her back to Homestead Pass. No time to think about dancing in Sam's arms last Friday night. Or to consider that she hadn't seen him since a brief greeting in church on Sunday and the fact that she missed him.

The realization took her by surprise. She'd been gone for five years, and during that time, she'd missed Sam. She'd missed her friend. But her career had taken off and there was no time for regrets. She'd made the cold, hard decision that breaking off their engagement was the best for both of them.

What she felt now was different. Missing him meant longing for his quick wit, his smiles and gestures that showed he cared, even as he fought hard not to care.

She'd taken Sam for granted all those

years. What did she want from him now that she was back?

She didn't know, but their growing friendship was a good place to start.

Liv put her upper-body strength into the dough. Knead, fold and turn. Knead, fold and turn. She could do this with her eyes closed. Repeating the process until the mound became supple and smooth.

Without warning, lightning soared once again, accompanied by a loud crack. Liv jumped, knocking her phone off the shelf into a small hill of flour on the prep table.

Lunging for the device, she managed to dust her apron with white powder.

She sneezed, sending flour into the air like an old-fashioned Oklahoma dust bowl.

"God bless you."

Liv screamed. She whirled around and faced Sam.

He stood in the doorway near the back door, looking sheepish.

"You nearly gave me a heart attack." She gripped the counter with both hands and took slow breaths to calm her pounding heart.

"I'm sorry. I didn't mean to scare you." He handed her a towel.

She took it from him, swiped ineffectually at the flour on her face and sneezed again. "Excuse me."

"Bless you, again," he said.

Then he moved closer and took the towel from her hands. "It's all over you." He folded the fabric and carefully wiped her cheeks, her nose and then her chin as she stood frozen, mesmerized and dumbstruck.

She couldn't think and didn't dare move as he leaned perilously closer. Close enough that she could see the flecks of amber surrounding the irises of his blue eyes. She smelled peppermint on his breath as his lips inched nearer. In a heartbeat, she realized that she wanted his kiss more than she'd wanted anything in a long time.

Her nose began to twitch.

Liv quickly jumped away from Sam and turned her head.

"Achoo!"

The sneeze practically shook the room. She moved to the sink, where she splashed water on her face, washed her hands and dried them. Despite the coolness of the water, her face still burned. What was she thinking? She couldn't go around kissing men when she was in a committed relationship with her restaurant.

Yet, the reality of what almost had happened kept playing on a loop in her mind. She'd almost kissed Sam. He'd almost kissed her. And she'd sneezed like an elephant.

"Sorry," she murmured, unable to look at him.

"Me too."

Liv put a smile on her face and turned to greet him. "Welcome back. How was your trip? Things have been quiet here. It's been raining since yesterday. Thankfully, that hasn't stopped the tourists. Business is good next door, although I haven't had time to evaluate inventory. Oh, and someone from the *Elk City Daily News* dropped in. They want to interview me. Chef and entrepreneur, the reporter called me. That's scheduled for next week."

She stopped babbling and looked up at him.

A small smile lifted the corners of his mouth. "Good to see you, Liv."

"You too," she said softly. The words seemed inadequate. It was more than good to see him. His surprise visit was fast becoming the highlight of her week, and that wasn't supposed to happen.

"I was on my way home from the airport, and I saw the lights. I didn't mean to scare you. Next time, I'll call and let you know I'm out there first."

Next time.

"I was lost in my own little bread world," she said with a laugh. She reached for a bowl, buttered the sides and tucked the dough inside. Covering the container with clear wrap, she placed it in the fridge. "New recipe. Actually, old recipe, new chef. My grandmother's Italian crusty bread. Every now and then, if I catch my father in a good mood, I convince him to release a recipe from the vault." She smiled. "He's been in a good mood often these days."

"You're a chef. Why doesn't he give you all the recipes?"

She shook her head. "It's a control thing. The recipes are bread crumbs. He's been doing this since my mother passed."

"It ensures you keep him in your life."

Liv sighed as she processed the words. "I guess you're right. Sometimes I forget how alone he's been."

"You know, you're very fortunate to have such a rich heritage of recipes. That's written history for your descendants."

That would be true if she had any descendants. The Morettis were phasing out, while the Morgan family tree seemed to be just getting started.

Liv looked at Sam. "I've heard your grandfather talk about the Morgan family coming over from Ireland plenty of times."

Sam laughed. "Ah yes, the Morgans of County Limerick. We have a family crest and everything. I am truly blessed. However, if we had to live with our own cooking, the family tree wouldn't last long. Which makes me grateful for Bess."

Liv chuckled.

An awkward silence descended. Since she was talked out, the only solution was food.

"Are you hungry?" she asked. "I have spaghetti in the fridge."

"Sure," Sam said. "I'd never turn down Olivia Moretti food."

She heated up the spaghetti, added a couple slices of bread and a bottle of water, then placed everything on the prep table.

While he ate, she began to clean up her work area with a focus that she'd lacked all week. She scrubbed the cupboards and counters while sneaking peeks at Sam, who stood at the table, watching her.

"So The Inspired Kitchen had a good week too, you said."

"Yes." Liv turned and grimaced. "I'm sorry I don't have numbers for you. The good news is we've been swamped."

"No worries." He glanced at the stainless steel clock on the wall. "Do you always stay this late?"

"I should have gone home hours ago," Liv said. "But Eleanor and my father are usually watching television or working on a puzzle, and I hate interrupting."

"The Eleanor-Anthony romance flourishes?"

"Does it ever."

"Maybe you'll have yourself a stepmother soon."

She dropped the sponge in the soapy water and faced him. *A stepmother.*

"Are you okay with that?"

"Sure. I think so." She paused, thinking. Her gaze met his. "This whole thing has been so surreal. My father has gone from needy to—"

"Needed?"

Liv jerked back as the words practically slapped her in the face. "You're right. All my father wanted was to be needed. How did I miss that?"

It was becoming apparent that she'd been so wrapped up in her career that she'd missed a lot of unspoken cues from her father. Like the recipe issue.

"Don't be so hard on yourself. I'm outside of the situation. I can be objective."

"Maybe I should be hard on myself. I

should have figured it out. All I could see was his nagging." Liv gave a short laugh. "I should have noticed that he's stopped complaining about how much time I spend here. And I haven't had a lecture about my duty to the ranch in over a week."

"Maybe he realizes that this—" Sam's gaze took in the space around them "—makes you happy."

She gave a bitter laugh. "I doubt it. Once the blush of new romance wears off, he'll be back to his usual mantra about my legacy."

"Moretti's Farm-to-Table Bistro *is* your legacy, Liv."

Liv stared at him. Stunned. Yes. This was her legacy. She smiled and sniffed back tears of relief. Someone got it. "Thank you," she murmured.

"I only stated the obvious." He finished off the bread and dusted his hands. "How was opening weekend at the restaurant? I barely saw you in church and didn't have a chance to ask before I left town on Tuesday."

Liv tucked the towel in her hand into her

apron pocket. "A huge success. I think part of it may be the limited seating. There's no availability for walk-ins because the reservations are full." She grinned. "That makes snagging a table more attractive."

A smile lifted Sam's lips, and he shook his head. "Or maybe your food is that amazing."

Liv bit her lip, pleased at his words. "Do you think so?"

"Yeah. I do. Everywhere I go, someone is talking about your linguine or tiramisu. I was standing in line at the post office when I overheard a woman raving to her friends about your vegetable lasagna." He looked pointedly at his empty plate. "They're right."

Liv's heart soared. "I appreciate you sharing that. Sometimes I feel like I'm working in a void. Though tomorrow marks one week, and it's been a full house every night."

"Congratulations. I'm proud of you, my friend."

She took pleasure in his words. "Thank you. So why haven't you stopped in for a meal during business hours?" she asked. "Drew and Sadie came in last night for date night. Even Bess has stopped by."

"You've only been open a week, and I've been out of town."

Liv cocked her head and stared pointedly at him. "That's your excuse?"

He played with the label on the water bottle, then downed a mouthful. "I'm your landlord. I thought it was best to maintain a professional distance."

Liv raised a brow, taking a small bit of delight at his stumbling. "Do you want to try one more time?"

Sam took a deep breath. "Honestly, it seems weird to come in and sit by myself in a fancy restaurant."

"People do it all the time. It's no different than sitting at the coffee shop."

He grimaced. "It is different."

"Bring your grandfather."

Sam appeared to mull the idea over. "I could do that."

"Yes, you could."

He nodded. "What's on the menu? Anything I might like?"

Liv inhaled sharply "Anything you might like?" She handed him a copy of the current menu. "Subject to change, according to our locally sourced products."

"You know I'm teasing you, right?"

She wagged a finger. "Never mess with the chef in her own kitchen."

"Yes, Chef."

Weariness settled on her, and she reached for her phone. "It's late. I better get going." She put his plate in the dishwasher and did a quick inspection of the kitchen before taking off her apron.

"Thanks for feeding me." He grabbed his water bottle. "Let me walk you to your truck."

Shadows danced around them when Liv turned off the kitchen lights and followed Sam to the back door. After securing the lock, she stepped outside to the small courtyard. The air smelled crisp and fresh, providing temporary relief from the constant humidity of late. The rain had stopped, and a cool breeze weaved around them, ruffling Sam's hair.

It seemed strange to be standing here with Sam, yet right somehow.

"What are your plans for this space back here?" he asked.

Liv followed his gaze as he assessed the black, wrought iron bistro table and the chairs with bright yellow cushions, positioned next to a tall pot of lemongrass.

"I haven't decided. At first, I had all sorts of grand ideas. It makes sense to provide additional seating here, but it's become my private retreat and I'm loath to give it up. Sometimes sitting here with an espresso can mean the difference between a good day and a not-very-good day." She looked at him. "Does that make sense?"

"Sure it does. I feel that way about my front porch. I try to find a way to get on that porch a few times a week. There's nothing like God's glory revealed in a sunset to put everything into perspective."

"Yes," she breathed. "That's it, exactly. When I sit here, and spend a few minutes in prayer, the chaos flees and calm fills my soul."

Sam's black truck was parked next to

hers, and she moved along the brick pavers toward her vehicle. Liv unlocked her door and then turned, staring at him for a moment. The streetlamp illuminated him as he stood next to his truck, looking dependable and handsome and all sorts of other things she didn't dare allow herself to think about.

His blue eyes watched her intently.

"Have a good night, Sam," she finally said.

He held up the menu she'd given him and winked. "Yeah, I will. I'll be dreaming about pierogies and cannoli."

Liv smiled as she slid into her truck and started the engine. She released a sigh. Food would not be on her mind tonight.

No. She'd be dreaming about blue eyes and that almost kiss in her kitchen.

Chimes announced Sam's presence as he pulled open the door of The Inspired Kitchen.

"Is there something I can help you find?" A silver-haired woman smiled at him from the behind the register.

"No, thank you, ma'am. I'm just looking."

His gaze skimmed the displays, taking in the placement. He wasn't an expert, but he'd taken several marketing classes in college. Liv must have as well.

She understood how to draw a customer in. Placing lower-cost cute impulse buys near the entrance encouraged customers to step deeper into the store. He found himself tempted to pick up a few of the items himself. Bess sure would love the ceramic chicken salt-and-pepper shakers.

"Nice shop you have here," he said.

"It really is. All Miss Olivia's doing. If you have a moment, do check out the hand-crafted wood items we feature. The craftsmanship is amazing. They're selling faster than I can unbox them and get them on the shelf."

"Is that so?" Sam smiled at the compliment while he strolled up and down the aisles, stopping to admire his products, which had been placed at eye level, offering them the best opportunity to be examined. "What's your bestseller?"

"The charcuterie boards. Hands down.

The striped ones, made of different types of wood, are very popular."

"Good to know." He glanced at the name tag of the woman at the counter. The famous Jane Smith, who Liv had mentioned. Sam held out a hand. "I'm Sam Morgan. You look mighty familiar, ma'am."

"I'm a friend of your grandfather's. And I was the librarian at Homestead Pass Middle School for years."

He lowered his voice. "I'm not still in trouble for those library books, am I?"

"It's been twenty-five years, Mr. Morgan. I can assure you that all is forgiven," she said with a prim smile. "Let me know if you have any questions while you're here."

He turned to see Liv come into the shop from the back room, smiling. If she'd noticed that he'd been avoiding her since that moment in her kitchen when he'd almost kissed her she didn't acknowledge the fact. Maybe he'd imagined things, and it wasn't a moment at all because she sure looked perky and well-rested. The woman kept smiling like all was well in her world.

Well, good for her. He'd popped into the store because he wanted to see her. A cringeworthy admission, since he'd gone to all the trouble of creating a plan whereby he would never have to see her.

"Sam! Nice to see you maintaining those landlord boundaries."

Ah, there it was. She *had* noticed.

"Gramps and I were in town to grab the mail and pick up supplies for the ranch, and I thought I'd stop in to see what you had to offer in your fine emporium."

Liv leaned closer. "You mean you want to know how business is doing."

"That too."

"Mrs. Smith," Liv called. "How's business been?"

"Very well. We sold out of those hope chests, and there's been a run on the charcuterie boards."

"Nice," Sam said. "Bess told me she bought a new frying pan."

Liv raised a brow. "Do I need to say I told you so?"

Sam kept his mouth shut. He hadn't

come in to check on business. He knew how business was doing. Last night he'd done the books. She'd made more sales, but his profits exceeded hers nearly two to one, which left the problem of what he was going to do about it. He couldn't admit that after two weeks, he actually liked the partnership he'd gone into kicking and screaming. Especially after he'd recently shut her down when she'd suggested doing away with the challenge.

She'd been right, but it was too late to change things without tipping his hand to the fact that he had changed his mind. He liked the partnership. Not only did he like it but it made sense.

Sam had parked himself in his office the last few days and got caught up on obligations to accounting clients. He'd come to a new appreciation of what Liv was doing in the store. Hiring Jane Smith was an excellent decision. She was as meticulous as Liv, which meant the books reconciled.

Now that he was caught up, the evenings were devoted to crafting. Liv was right.

Consigning his products to the shop and leaving the everyday running of the store to others had been working in his favor. He was walking a fine line, juggling all aspects of his life. For now, all his spinning plates were happy.

Yeah, the fact was he wouldn't mind keeping things status quo. The other perk was he could stop by under the guise of a silent partner and landlord while he worked to figure out what he planned to do about his growing feelings for Liv.

"Sam, did you hear what I said?" Liv asked.

"Yeah. I like the idea."

She burst out laughing. "You didn't hear me. Did you?"

"Not a word."

He looked at her, noticing the summery dress that flattered her tanned and golden arms and shoulders. She wore her fancy-stitched red boots, and her dark curls were clipped to her nape with a silver barrette. "You're all gussied up for a Thursday morning, aren't you? What's the occasion?"

Maybe she had a date. That thought soured him in a jiffy, and he was sorry he'd asked.

"I think you might have been attempting to compliment me," Liv said. "Your delivery needs some work. I'm dressed up because the reporter from the *Elk City Daily News* was here this morning."

"Reporter?"

Liv grinned, her eyes flashing with excitement. "The interview. Remember, I told you about it last week when you got back from California?"

"I guess I forgot." Fact was he didn't remember much except nearly kissing Liv.

"There was even a photographer who took pictures of the shop and the restaurant." Liv glanced out the front window. "In fact, you just missed them."

"You better hope Gramps doesn't see them. He'll bend their ear for sure."

"Gus? Why?"

"He's been trying to get the local papers to cover the Homestead Pass Annual Fishing Derby for years. The press doesn't think it's newsworthy since there's no cash prize. Gramps gets fired up once a year about it." He chuckled. "That cranky editor of the *Homestead Pass Daily Journal* threatened to have him arrested if he goes in the newspaper office again."

"I had no idea." She lifted her brows and glanced around before inching closer. "As I was saying and you weren't hearing, I need more inventory. You assured me when we started this partnership that inventory would not be a problem."

"It won't be a problem. Inventory is at the top of my to-do list." He glanced toward the door, recalling that he left Gramps at the Hitching Post. "Gotta run." With a nod to Jane Smith, he exited the store.

He cut through the parking lot of the inn and strode down the sidewalk to the Hitching Post as fast as he could. Gramps was waiting beneath the store's canopy with "impatient" all over his face as he snacked on a beef jerky.

"Where'd you disappear to?" Gus asked. "You used to do that when you were six years old. I'd turn around and you were gone. I would have thought you'd outgrown that by now."

"How do you feel about dinner at Liv's place sometime?" Sam asked.

"You buying?"

"Yeah. What about for your birthday?"

"Aw, you know Bess always makes me a special meal for my birthday."

He fought a chuckle. "Gramps, when you get to be mature, you can have more than one birthday celebration. This would be just you and me."

"Mature." He laughed. "Okay, I'll bite. What's the catch?"

"There is no catch. Why are you so suspicious?"

"I'm not suspicious. I'm careful. If more people were careful, the world would be a better place."

Sam rolled his eyes good-naturedly and started walking toward the truck. "No more Dr. Pepper for you, pal. You're all wound up." Dr. Pepper remained a standing thing between him and Gramps. After too much caffeine, his grandfather couldn't locate the reins for his mouth.

Gus shrugged. "When did you start selling your stuff in Olivia's shop?"

Sam nearly tripped over his feet at the question. He turned around slowly. "How did you know about that?"

"I stopped in the store when they opened and said hello to Jane. Looked around and was gobsmacked to see your handiwork. Mighty fine, Sam. I'm proud of you."

"Aw, thanks, Gramps." His heart warmed at the recognition. Then Sam frowned. "Um, Gramps. How did you know it was mine?"

"Why are you asking me these ridiculous questions? Your initials are on them."

"You didn't say anything did you?" Sam asked.

"I would have, 'cept Jane got busy with a customer, and I had to leave. Truth is, I forgot about it until now."

He released a breath of relief. "Gramps, do me a favor and continue to forget about it. Would you?" Sam took a deep breath and offered up a silent prayer. Asking his grandfather to keep a secret was like asking a bucking bronc to play nice.

His grandfather shrugged. "If you say so."

Sam started toward the truck again. "I do."

"Does Olivia know it's your stuff?"

"Yeah, she knows."

"I'm a little confused here," his grandfather said. "What's the problem?"

"Give me some time, and I'll explain it to you." He held the door open for his grandfather and then hopped in and fastened his seat belt.

When they hit the outskirts of town, his grandfather turned toward him.

"So she knows about your woodworking, but she doesn't know about the house. Do I have that straight?"

"Gramps." As the Morgan patriarch, his grandfather specialized in pushing buttons.

"Don't 'Gramps' me. You spent a year working on that house. Put in sweat equity and your last dollar and you never told her?"

"It wouldn't have mattered."

"You don't know that."

Sam tightened his hands on the steering wheel. Gramps didn't get it. If the ring and the proposal didn't matter, why would the house?

"What's going on with you and Olivia these days?" his grandfather continued.

"Nothing. Not a thing." Sam jacked up the air-conditioning.

"No risk, no reward. No pain, no gain. No guts, no glory."

"That's all you got?" Sam asked eyes wide with surprise. More than once, he'd seen his grandfather offer a sage nod before dishing Drew an hour of advice on his love life.

Gus lifted an eyebrow. "Son, I've got news for you. That's all you need."

His grandfather might be right, but he wasn't prepared to test the premise. Sam gave a slight shake of his head. Nope. There was no way he was interested in being dumped twice in a lifetime.

Chapter Nine

Sam rubbed mineral oil into the wood and assessed the grain from all angles. He wasn't happy with the corners of the cutting board. Tomorrow he'd run it through the router and round out the corners.

But he was done for today. He removed his apron and hung it on a peg next to the framed photo of himself and his father.

Woodworking was a skill that took a lifetime to master. It had turned out that once Liv left, he had plenty of time on his hands. He'd built up quite an inventory. Now he had to produce on demand, which was a whole different animal and not nearly as therapeutic.

He grabbed a water bottle from the small workshop refrigerator and headed toward his house. There was still time to enjoy the sunset from the porch, so he took the steps in two strides and sank into one of the glossy black rocking chairs he'd crafted himself.

The slow motion of the rocker lulled him, but the heat nearly did him. He took a swig of cold water, splashing some over his face to ease the humidity of the day. The temperatures wouldn't drop as evening approached, now that it was nearly summer. No, Oklahoma in summer meant two temperatures. Hot and hotter.

The sunset, however, did not disappoint, arriving in shades of gold and amber, with fingers of red stretching along the horizon, creating a backdrop for the cluster of peach trees he'd planted.

It would have been nice to share this view with someone.

Who would have thought that he'd build a home only to live in it alone? Back then, he'd been foolishly optimistic and buoyed by love. The love was long gone, but the house remained. He'd built it on a solid foundation. The house remained a warning against future foolhardy decisions.

Yeah, he'd dodged a bullet there. Liv wasn't marriage material. She was way too stubborn and bossy, though she sure could cook. He'd give her that. And she was sweet, kind, generous, with a heart for the Lord.

Sam groaned at the wayward direction of his thoughts. He needed a dog. Now that his brothers had moved out, the place was empty. Maybe two dogs. And a cat.

His phone dinged, and he pulled it out. Drew had sent a video of his baby boy and his curly-haired nearly two-year-old daughter.

They had to be the cutest kids he'd ever seen. Despite the late-night diaper changes and colic, he'd never seen his brother happier. Maybe it was years on the ranch, assisting hundreds of births, but Sam longed for a house full of kids. Young ones that he could teach ranching or woodworking to, or whatever their dream was.

Before he could set the phone down, it rang—a number he didn't recognize.

"Morgan here."

"Oh, thank goodness. Sam, this is Loretta Moretti. I'm trying to find Olivia. I'm certain she's at the restaurant. However, the phone there is going directly to voice mail, and she isn't answering her cell."

"Have you tried her friend Robyn?"

"No, it's Sunday. Robyn is in Oklahoma City with her fiancé." Loretta's voice trembled.

"What's going on?" he asked, sensing trouble.

"Oh, Sam, Anthony is in the hospital." She paused as if to collect herself. "I thought maybe you could tell Liv and then drive her here."

"Which hospital? Is he going to be okay?"

"I'm praying so. Elk City General. They say he had a heart attack."

"Okay, Loretta. I'll get Liv. Don't worry about that." He swallowed. "I'll be praying too."

"Don't let her drive. Promise me that."

"You can count on me."

"I know I can. Thank you." Hands shaking, Sam nearly dropped the phone as he turned off the lights in the shop.

They'd weathered many crises together, he and Liv, and he knew that she'd be a rock, no matter what was going on. Sam washed his face and threw on clean clothes before jumping into his dually and heading to town, praying all the way.

His thoughts were all over the map as he drove. Losing his own parents at seventeen had been agony. Liv had supported him through that tragedy, and he had been there when her mother passed only a few years later.

Their past and their future didn't matter tonight. All that mattered was being the friend she needed.

Sam drove slowly past the parking lot that separated the inn and the Snodgrass Building and spotted her red truck out front. He parked and banged on the restaurant door.

Immediately, the lights in the dining room came on. A shade rose, and Liv looked at him, puzzled, before she opened the door. "Well, you didn't scare me this time." She smiled. "What's up?"

"Where's your phone? You didn't answer."

Liv patted her back pocket. "Oh, I must have left it in the truck. I've been busy changing up the table decor for the upcoming week." She nodded toward the dining room. "What do you think?"

He glanced around at the space. The schoolhouse fixtures overhead bounced soft light off the unfinished brick wall, casting a golden glow on the room. The dining tables were dressed in creamy white linen with hunter green napkins and bud vases filled with gerbera daisies.

"Beautiful. Liv."

Come on, Sam, tell her.

She looked at his face and tensed. "What's wrong?"

He hesitated, searching for a gentle delivery. There was none.

"Your dad is in the hospital. Loretta says he had a heart attack."

Liv swayed and grabbed the edge of the

hostess stand for support. She stared at the floor, her breathing measured. Then she straightened, pulling herself together.

"Did she give you any details?"

"No. They took him to Elk City."

She walked back toward the kitchen and returned with a purse. "Thanks, Sam." The words seemed like a dismissal.

"I'm driving you."

"That's not necessary. I can drive. It's only fifteen miles away."

"Liv, I'm driving you. Give me your keys, and I'll grab your phone."

She acquiesced far too easily, digging in her purse and offering him the keys, her face grim.

"Meet you at the dually." He raced down the sidewalk to the parking lot, opened her truck and grabbed her phone off the front seat.

When he strode back toward the restaurant, he found Liv standing on the sidewalk beneath the streetlamp, her brown eyes huge in her pale face as she stared into the night, looking lost.

"Truck's open," he called.

She nodded and climbed in, then put on her seat belt before wrapping her arms around herself.

"I should have stayed home tonight," Liv murmured. "But Eleanor and my father were in the kitchen making pizza. I felt like a third wheel." She held her hands together tightly and sighed. "I should have stayed home."

"Stop. Don't do that to yourself. You know better." He reached out and put a hand over hers. "Anthony is tougher than both of us, and I know the Lord hears our prayers. So let's pray."

Liv nodded.

"Lord, we thank you for taking care of Anthony. Please keep him safe and heal that big heart of his. Amen."

"Amen," Liv said softly.

He fastened his seat belt, backed out and headed west down Route 66 to Elk City.

"I should call my aunt," Liv said. "Except I feel like I'm in a fog that I can't crawl out of."

"Do you want me to pull over?" Sam asked.

"No. Keep going." She picked up her phone from the seat and punched in a number. "Zia, are you at the hospital?" Liv looked out the window, eyes narrowed.

"Yes, we're about ten miles away."

"Praise God. Okay, thanks. I love you. See you soon."

Liv stared down at the cell. "He was admitted to Elk City General's cardiac care unit. His cardiologist decided not to transport him to Oklahoma City since he's stable." She looked at him. "Stable. That's the word she used. That's good, right?"

"Very good."

She released a breath. "Loretta will meet us in the waiting room. They haven't allowed her to go in."

"We're almost there."

For miles, Liv stared out into the darkness, her brow furrowed. As they approached the outskirts of Elk City, she turned in her seat.

"Thanks for being here, Sam."

"Hey, that's what friends are for. You'd have done the same for me."

"Should I call Eleanor?" she asked.

"Let's wait until we get there and talk to the doctors." He hit the turn indicator and drove through the hospital entrance and into visitor parking. "This way," he said after they stepped out and crossed the parking lot.

"Do you know where we're going?" she asked.

"Yeah, Bess had a cardiac incident last year. I visited her here." The facility was fairly new and boasted easy access, generous use of natural lighting and sparkling floors.

Loretta met them in the waiting room. Like Liv, her brown eyes were marked with concern.

"Olivia. Sam. I'm so glad to see your faces." She wrapped her arms around Liv and offered Sam a kiss on the cheek.

"Have you been updated?" Liv asked.

"A little." Loretta shrugged. "His cardiologist came out and gave me medical-speak that I didn't completely understand, so the nurse kindly translated." She sighed. "They're watching his cardiac enzymes. Please, do not ask me what those are. Right now the cardiac team is evaluating to determine the amount of damage his heart muscle incurred."

"I guess the good news is that he's right where he should be, with professionals taking care of him," Liv said. Her hand still gripped her aunt's arm.

"Exactly," Loretta said.

"Can we see him?" Liv asked softly. She wiped at her eyes. The gesture nearly broke Sam's heart. Liv never cried.

"Not yet," her aunt said. "It's a small area, with technicians, nurses and doctors buzzing around. Visiting is extremely limited." She sat down on a plastic chair. "We may as well get comfortable."

Sam looked between both women. "I'm going to take a ride out to Eleanor's place before it gets late and bring her here. I'll call her son on the way and update him."

"Oh, Sam. Thank you," Loretta said.

He nodded. "Can I bring either of you anything back?"

"A few water bottles would be good," Liv said.

"Will do." Sam started back the way

they'd come and heard Liv call his name. He turned as she caught up with him.

"You've never let me down, Sam." She sniffed, her eyes still moist. "I am so grateful to have you back in my life."

It killed him to see the pain in her eyes as she spoke. He knew what it was like to lose a loved one, and he worked to bite back his own emotion.

"Liv, I'm not looking for your gratitude. Anthony is my friend. Just as you are."

She swallowed and nodded.

"See you soon." He kissed the top of her head and turned away, his heart aching for her.

"Please, Lord. Take care of Liv's daddy," he murmured.

"I never want to see you in a hospital bed with IV tubes and wires hooked up to you ever again, Papà," Liv said. She slid a plate of muffins on the table and turned on the burner under the tea kettle.

"Me either," her father said. "Getting out of that hospital is the best Father's Day present a man can have." He glanced around the kitchen from his seat at the table.

"I couldn't agree more," Liv returned.

"Here, here," Loretta said from her spot across the room where she sipped espresso.

Liv's throat tightened as she recalled the events of the last week. Her father's hospitalization had tested her faith and her ability to let go and delegate. She, Loretta and Eleanor had tag-teamed at the hospital to ensure someone was always with her father.

And Sam had checked in, either in person or by phone, each day. The gesture left her with a reminder of how much kindness there was in his cowboy heart. It also left her wondering if she would be able to keep from falling in love with him all over again.

"What are these?" Anthony asked. He eyeballed the muffins with suspicion.

"Robyn dropped off her special bran muffins before she left for the day."

"Bran muffins?" Her dad grimaced and quickly surveyed the stove. "When will the pasta be ready?"

"Today we're having heart-healthy chicken piccata, salad and fruit," Liv said.

"What?" Disgust had him pulling his brows together. "Pasta is tradition. We always have pasta with meatballs on Sunday."

"There's nothing wrong with pasta, but not every Sunday," Liv said. "Moderation."

Scowling, he turned to Loretta. "Did you agree to this?"

"I'm standing with Olivia," Loretta returned. "You're outnumbered."

"Ha! I've always been outnumbered."

"Yes, but we've always let you think you were in charge. No more." Loretta smiled at her brother.

Confronting her father had never been easy. Most of her life Liv had avoided such interaction. That was about to change. She would push him, because she loved him and never wanted to experience the pain of the last week again. Especially when it was preventable.

"Fine." He released a dramatic sigh and for a moment Liv was taken aback by the acquiescence.

Loretta cocked her head toward the door. "I hear the dryer beeping." She looked at Liv. "I'm cooking today."

"Thank you, Zia."

"Did you invite Eleanor to my heart-healthy lunch?" her father asked when Loretta left.

"Of course. And I think we can all agree that Eleanor is wonderful." Liv meant the words. Eleanor had remained calm and reassuring, offering words of comfort and prayers when needed.

Anthony was all smiles, then he eyed Liv cautiously. "I had nothing but time to think while I was in that hospital bed for a week. At night, when everyone went home, and I was alone, I thought about the future."

"I'm sorry you had to go through that." Liv hugged him. "Tell me what you thought about."

"You, and your mother and Sam and Eleanor."

Liv raised a brow, patiently waiting for him to continue and a little concerned about what was coming.

"I'm sad that you and Sam didn't get

married. You two could have taken over the ranch when I retire. Now you must do it alone."

Liv sighed. "I'm not my mother. I cannot give up my career for the ranch."

Surprise filled her father's eyes and his jaw slacked. "Is that what you think?" He shook his head. "Your mother didn't give up ballet for the ranch. She escaped dance to come to America and be my wife. That was her heart's desire."

Liv frowned. "You used to tell me those stories."

He shook his head, more adamantly this time. "Your mother would never speak ill of her family. But she had been dancing since she was three years old. She was ready to leave that world behind and her parents wouldn't hear of it."

Liv found herself stunned by the information. At the same time, the insight gave her the courage to be brutally honest with her father.

"Papà, I am not going to manage the ranch. Ever. I am a chef," she said. "A very good chef. The restaurant is my dream, and it makes me happy."

"I want you to be happy." He paused, his gaze heavy with sadness. "But what will happen to M&M?"

"We'll figure it out," she said softly. "Together. We'll figure it out."

"And Sam?" He tilted his head to watch her closely.

She took her father's hand. "Sam and I are making our way back to friends. I want you to promise not to interfere."

"Fine. Fine." Anthony's dark eyes rounded, a guilty expression crossing his face. "Does that mean Sam can't come to supper? I already invited him."

Of course he already invited him. Liv nearly laughed aloud. It would be good to see Sam again. She hadn't had a chance to thank him for taking her to the hospital. And truth be told, she missed him.

"Sam is always welcome here, Papà."

"What do think about me getting married again?"

She jerked up in her chair. "What?"

"I'm going to ask Eleanor to marry me."

She stilled. "You only recently started seeing her."

"I've known her for years." He raised his shoulders. "I'm not getting any younger. No need to wait, is there?"

Surprise turned to acceptance as Liv processed the idea.

"No. No need to wait." She smiled, realizing she was delighted for her father. This was what her mother would want as well. "Papà, I'm happy for you."

"Thank you, my beautiful daughter." He grinned. "And do you approve of Sam as my best man?"

Liv laughed. "I absolutely approve." Sam and her father had been close until she left town. She regretted that she had made the relationship between the two men awkward.

Her father nodded, as though very pleased. "And did I tell you? Eleanor's son and daughter-in-law are about to have a baby."

"That's a bonus," Liv said with a laugh.

A smile lit up Anthony's face. "Right? I marry Eleanor and get a grandbaby to spoil. Win-win." He laughed. "Don't tell Eleanor I said that, and don't tell her I'm going to pop the question."

"I won't." She tilted her head. "When are you going to propose?"

"I already invited her to dinner at your restaurant on Wednesday. You make the reservation."

"Wednesday! You were just discharged."

"I read those discharge instructions. There was nothing about not going to my daughter's restaurant." He pointed a finger. "Make the reservation."

"Fine, but Eleanor is driving. You haven't been cleared to drive."

"I can work with that. But remember what the doctor said. My lungs are better, and I can have that procedure soon. Things are looking up."

Liv nodded. That was an unexpected bit of good news. "You keep following the doctor's instructions and I'll keep praying. Deal?"

"Deal."

The doorbell rang, and Liv stood.

"Are we done?" her father asked.

"For now." She headed to the front door, pulled it open and ushered Sam into the foyer.

Sam shot her a wary look. "You knew I was invited to lunch and to watch the game, right?" He handed her a paper grocery sack.

"Yes." She looked him up and down and tried not to stare, but it was difficult to ignore how handsome he looked today. His pale blue cotton dress shirt brought out the blue in his eyes.

He assessed her outfit, brows raised. "You look like you're in high school."

Liv glanced down at her old T-shirt and torn jeans and decided not to change her clothes. "Sunday casual." She was getting more and more relaxed around him, like the old days.

"A good look for you."

"Thanks," she murmured. Liv unfolded the top of the grocery sack, head down, so he wouldn't see her face warming. "What's this?"

"Your father asked me to pick up a gallon of Neapolitan ice cream on my way over."

Liv groaned. He'd done it again. "I tell him sorbet, frozen yogurt, gelato or 'light' ice cream, and he tells you to bring Neapolitan." She looked at her father's coconspirator. "He's on a very strict diet now."

Sam held up a white pastry bag in his other hand and offered an apologetic look. "I guess that means the maple bars are out too. I drove to Elk City for the ones he requested. Your father has a very discerning palate, doesn't he?"

Liv's mouth fell open in surprise. She snatched the white bag from him. "I'll hide the ice cream behind the frozen vegetables in the freezer. The maple bars are now mine."

"Good plan," he said. "I already ate two on my way over."

They stared awkwardly at each other for a moment. Liv searched for something to say. All she could come up with was *I haven't seen you in a week. What's with that, Sam? And why do you look so good? Are you trying to confuse me?*

"Thanks for visiting my father in the hospital," she finally said.

"Oh, he told you?"

"Yes. I was sorry to have missed you." She shifted the ice cream before her left forearm froze.

"Yeah. Busy week. Those special orders are taking up my extra hours. I'll drop off more inventory soon," he said. "Don't worry."

"I wasn't concerned."

"No?" Sam nodded, his attention focused on something on the wall behind her. "Restaurant doing well? Any problems I should know about? I mean, as your landlord."

"Nope. Everything is great."

"Is that Sam?" her father called.

"Yes, Papà."

"Send him into the living room. We have wedding plans to discuss."

"You better get in there." Liv pointed to the living room.

"What wedding plans?" Sam asked. Panic laced his voice.

"Relax. He's talking about his wedding. Not yours."

"Oh, good." He smiled. "Nice talking to you, Liv."

"Yes, a real treat," she muttered.

Liv stood in the doorway of the living room for a moment, as the two men greeted each other with much fanfare. Five years ago, this male bonding terrified her. She'd been threatened by what she saw as a conspiracy to steal her dreams. Now she understood no one could steal her dreams unless she let them.

Besides, she'd drawn a line in the Oklahoma red dirt today with her father. Things were going to be different.

As for Sam? He was back in her life. Sam was her friend and that was where she wanted him.

Or was she lying to herself?

Liv peeked into the white bag and smiled. She tiptoed down the hall and headed to the kitchen to eat a maple bar and mull that over.

Things were out of control. Sam shook his head as he sat in his truck outside Drew's house. Today was Tuesday and instead of cleaning up the stack of paperwork on his desk, he'd spent the better part of the morning in Elk City at the jewelers picking up a ring Anthony had special ordered. It was the same store where he'd bought Liv's ring.

While he'd definitely agreed to run the errand for Liv's father, he hadn't realize how stepping into the jewelers would bring back a slew of memories.

Sam leaned back in his seat.

So many memories.

The night he'd popped the question slipped into his mind. Liv was so animated, talking nonstop about her latest position as assistant to the pastry chef. It only seemed appropriate to pull out the ring as she finished eating dessert.

Her brown eyes had become soft and misty as she said yes to his proposal. The most nerve-wracking thirty seconds of his life.

They had talked about marriage in some nebulous future. But he was ready, and he hoped marriage meant she'd travel a little less, though they hadn't discussed the topic.

That was his first mistake and his last.

He hit a palm against the steering wheel.

Why had he agreed to that stupid bargain? The decision was not only arrogant but a massive error in judgment. He'd been so confident that he could distance himself from Liv physically and emotionally.

Wrong.

Setting himself up for disaster. That was what he was doing.

Now he was not only tangled up with Liv, but with her whole family again. He stared up at Drew's house. Hopefully his big brother could offer some advice.

Sam had called Drew to say he was coming, but the phone had gone to voice mail. This would be a quick visit. Long enough for his brother to knock some sense into him.

He took the steps two at a time and then stood there. Did he ring the bell or knock? Either could wake a sleeping baby. Maybe this was a bad idea too. Sam turned away just as the front door swung open. He glanced over his shoulder to see Liv standing behind the screen.

Good night! Every time he turned around,

he ran into the woman. His world was shrinking, or maybe his days were numbered.

"Hey, Sam. I saw your truck pull up." She opened the screen and stepped outside, looking cute and cheerful. He tried not to notice. "Are you okay? You seemed to be having an argument with yourself in the truck."

"Singing along to the music." Sam offered a weak smile.

"Must have been a good song," she murmured.

"I was looking for Drew," Sam said. "Had a few questions." He paused. "What are you doing here?"

"I'm babysitting. Drew and Sadie took Mae to Tulsa for her annual cardiac checkup. I'm staying with little Andy."

"I didn't see your car."

"That's because Drew picked me up. My truck is in the shop again. Time for a new one like yours."

Sam straightened, prepared to defend his purchase. "It's not brand-new. Though it does have all the bells and whistles which hooked me. That baby has a seat warmer and GPS guidance that talks to me in Spanish."

Liv frowned. "Do you know Spanish?"

He gestured with his thumb and forefinger. *"Un poquito."*

"You're kidding, right? How do you get to your destination if you don't understand the language?"

"Nope. Not kidding. It's sort of a game I play, teaching myself the language." He smiled. "I've got 'make a U-turn' in Spanish memorized."

Liv started laughing. The sound wrapped around him, melting the last of the ice he'd packed his heart in for safekeeping. "That's hilarious."

For a moment, he simply stared at her.

This. This was the problem. His brain went on vacation when Liv was around.

"I, ah… Nice of you to babysit," he finally said.

"They were going to take Andy along, and I might have insisted." She glanced up at the sky, where a relentless sun beat down on them. "It's hot out here. Come on in."

"Oh, I don't know. I should come back later." Sam turned to leave.

"You're already here, and I made ricotta cookies."

He stopped and slowly turned back. "Loretta's recipe?"

"Yes. I frosted them and put sprinkles on top." Liv grinned with certainty. Yeah, she had his number.

"You drive a hard bargain," Sam said.

He stepped into the house and glanced around. Drew and Sadie's home was spacious yet cozy. So far, he'd only mastered the "spacious" part at his house. His place could use a decorator's touch, but he'd lost interest in that once he moved in.

The plaintive wails of his nephew filled the air. "Uh-oh, he knows Uncle Sam is here."

Liv chuckled. "He's hungry, and no doubt needs a diaper change." She headed down the hall toward the crying baby.

"Mind if I observe?" Sam asked.

"Not at all."

Sam had barely settled himself against the door jamb before Liv had the diaper changed and the blanketed bundle cradled in the nook of her arm, despite protests. A few soothing whispers and a soft kiss on his cheek, and the baby quieted.

"Nice job," he said.

"Like riding a horse." She smiled. "All those years I spent babysitting in high school for extra money. My father never believed in free rides. I had to earn my way."

He followed her into the kitchen, where she moved the baby to her shoulder and reached into the refrigerator for a bottle.

"I can hold him while you fix that bottle."

"Sure. That would be helpful."

He carefully took the baby from her arms, his fingers touching hers at the exchange. For a moment, he tried to imagine a world where caring for a baby with Liv was his reality. His heart ached for what might have been.

Sam knew he ought to keep his mouth shut, but the gate had creaked open on what-ifs, and his brain demanded a few answers.

"When we had premarital counseling with the pastor, you were noncommittal about having kids," he said.

She pulled the bottle from the pan of water and gently shook it before testing the temperature of the milk. Her forehead remained scrunched in thought. Then she turned and pointed at him with the bottle.

"This discussion stays here. I've already had the boundaries talk with my father about interfering in my personal life. If he hears anything about grandchildren, I'll have to sit him down for another chat."

"On my honor. Between you and me." The baby stared up at Sam, blue eyes inquisitive, as though he was invested in the conversation. A conversation Sam never thought he'd be having with Liv.

"Have a seat," she said. "You can feed the baby while I make coffee."

"Me?" He looked down at Andy in alarm. "We established that you're the professional."

Liv gave him a sweet smile and handed

him the bottle. "I have complete confidence in you."

Sam hesitantly accepted the bottle. "Great. That makes one of us." The baby latched on to the bottle, which was a surprise. Someday when the kid grew up a little more, he'd thank him for not making a fool of Uncle Sam in front of Liv.

"I deny it to my father, but now that I'm not traveling, I can see myself with a family someday. What about you? You always said you wanted a houseful. Has that changed?"

"Nope. I still want at least four, like my parents."

She laughed. "Two isn't enough, and three messes with the dynamics. Four is perfect."

He smiled, surprised she'd remembered his rationale. "Yep. My brothers and I would pair up according to who was mad at who on any given day. You always have a buddy or a partner in crime when there are four."

"I always wanted a partner in crime."

He nodded. "I know. But you've said you

were never lonely." He recalled pictures he'd seen at her house of Liv as a child with her big brown eyes and wavy hair.

"No. My mother was a stay-at-home mom and taught me so much—ballet, a love of music, and cooking. Still, it wasn't the same as a sibling."

He checked the bottle before looking up at Liv. "Would you stay home if you had kids?"

She paused. "Owning a business means unpredictable hours. A great deal of thought and planning would have to go into a schedule that would work for myself and my theoretical family."

"You've thought about it, then."

"A bit." She eyed him. "What about you? Would you stay at home if you had kids?"

He chuckled at the gotcha question. "I could."

She grinned. "Good answer."

"What about that coffee?" he asked.

"I already made the coffee. Right before you showed up. It was a ruse to get you to feed your nephew."

Sam looked down at the baby and then up at her. "Well played."

"I thought so."

He stared at her. "You're different, Liv."

"Different, how?"

"I don't know. You're clear about what you want."

"When I decided to come home, I made a promise that I was going to settle things with my father once and for all. I may have finally accomplished that."

"It's not easy. I get that. My brothers and I watched our dad go after his lifelong plan to start a cattle ranch. Like your dad, he built the Lazy M from nothing. But he never let us feel like it was an obligation. I never felt like I had to give up my life for the ranch."

"Yes. That's the thing. That's the whole reason I ran, Sam. I believed at the time that my mother compromised everything she wanted for love. I felt like a failure because I couldn't too."

"But I never asked you to."

"I know that now. I didn't then." She shook her head. "The thing is, I was wrong about my mother. My father set me straight. She gave up her career by choice. I never knew that."

"Puts a different light on things, huh?"

"Completely. Would it have changed how I felt five years ago? Probably not," she finished gently.

Andy's bottle complete, the baby began to fuss, and Liv scooped him from Sam's arms. Her hair brushed Sam's face as she did, and he inhaled the intoxicating fragrance of baby and woman.

He stood, suddenly feeling claustrophobic. Memories were starting to close in on him. Memories of what might have been. Would he and Liv have had a family by now? That thought haunted him as he sat in his brother's house.

"I should get back. I don't usually play hooky in the middle of the day."

"Grab some cookies before you leave," Liv said.

"I can do that." He picked up a handful from the plate on the table and then met her gaze.

"This was good, Sam. We should talk more often."

Sam nodded. They should have talked more often five years ago.

"I'll tell Drew you stopped by. You had questions for him, right?"

"No need. I figured out the answers myself."

Yep, he sure had. He'd arrived at his brother's front door confused about his feelings for Liv. No longer. He'd crossed the line from confusion to complete clarity.

He'd lost his heart and maybe his peace of mind too.

Sam Morgan, you are in serious trouble.

Chapter Ten

Sam followed as Liv led his grandfather to a table. "Is this satisfactory, Gus?" she asked.

"This is the most satisfactory table I've seen in a long time," Gus said. He sat down, unbuttoned his suit coat and adjusted his tie with a grin.

"Thanks, Liv." Sam sat as well. He took the menu she offered and covertly assessed the woman. This was her world, her restaurant, and this was the first time he'd seen her in her role as Olivia Moretti, restaurateur. Polished, professional, confident and commanding. That was what she exuded tonight. She wore a navy dress with her hair pulled back in a fancy twist at the back of her head, which only added to her agency. He found himself mesmerized and a bit intimidated.

Wasn't it just yesterday that they were talking at Drew's house? She'd had spit-up formula on her shoulder and smelled like baby lotion. She was just as beautiful tonight, but in a different way.

"Don't you think so, Sam?" his grandfather asked.

"I do," Sam said.

Liv laughed. "You didn't hear a word he said. Did you?"

"Aw, Gramps has lots of words. I can't be expected to hear them all."

She laughed again and the sound warmed him. "You're not in the kitchen?" he asked.

"Robyn and my aunt have that honor." She smiled generously. "Your server will be here shortly to take your beverage order. Remember, you're my special guests this evening. Dinner is on the house."

She stepped away and headed toward the kitchen. Sam's gaze followed. This was her dream and she had nailed it. He was so proud of her.

"On the house. What did you do to deserve that?" Gus asked.

"It's on the house because it's your birthday."

"You don't say? Well, now I'm sorry I complained so much about wearing my church clothes." He looked around. "This is a nice place. Not too fancy schmancy. I like it."

"I agree. Thanks for being my date."

"Your date?" His grandfather chuckled and leaned forward. "Here's a tip. Next time, pick someone prettier to share a romantic table with candlelight. And remember, this is our first date, so mind your manners."

Sam laughed. It was never a dull moment with his grandfather. He didn't dare admit that this actually was his first date in a long time.

A server came by to fill their water glasses and take their drink orders.

"Water is fine for me," Sam said.

"I'll take a Dr. Pepper. Thank you."

"Go easy on that stuff tonight, Gramps," Sam joked.

"Aw, it's my birthday. It's not every year that I turn eighty-two."

"You're right. I'm pretty sure you're the most senior senior citizen in Homestead Pass now."

"Not true by a long shot. Though being mature does have its perks. I get free coffee on Wednesdays at the coffee shop and a ten percent discount once a month at the grocery store. That adds up, you know."

"It does."

"What'll we order?" His grandfather picked up his menu and studied it like the newspaper. "I'm thinking about having dessert first. I'm always too full to eat dessert in a restaurant, and there's no raiding the refrigerator for leftovers at midnight like at home." He pointed to the menu. "What's that say? *Panna Cotta?*"

"It's a custard," Sam said. "You know, Gramps. We can take dessert home."

Gus's brows rose. "Whoa. We're going whole hog tonight, aren't we?"

"Yes, sir. We are, and we deserve it."

Sam was enjoying his evening with his grandfather. He should have done something like this a long time ago. Leave it to Liv to make the suggestion.

Gus grinned. "You just opened the chute, and the horse is out. I'm getting the four-cheese ravioli and those zucchini fritters."

"How about stuffed mushroom appetizers?"

"What do you suppose they stuff them with?"

"I don't know. Let's step out of our comfort zone. You know. No guts, no glory. No risk, no reward."

Gus started laughing. "I've heard that somewhere before."

Sam was more than impressed when their dinner appeared soon after they'd ordered. After a quick prayer, they both dug in.

"That's a beautiful thing." Gus sat back in his chair and admired his plate of ravioli. "Don't tell Bess how much I'm enjoying this. Maybe don't mention this bread either." He reached for another slice of the warm, crusty Italian loaf.

"I won't, but you might have to explain how you dipped your tie in that sauce."

His grandfather looked down and grimaced. "You can't take me anywhere, can you?"

A smiling Liv walked over and assessed their plates. "How is your dinner? Is there anything you need?"

"Olivia, everything is delicious," Gus said. "You have done your daddy proud with this restaurant."

"What a lovely thing to say. Thank you."

Loretta came up to the table behind Liv, dressed in her white chef uniform with her name stitched on the jacket pocket. "Gentlemen, good to see you. Happy birthday, Gus." She put a hand on Liv's shoulder and nodded toward the kitchen.

"Excuse us," Liv said. Both women left, and minutes later, the lights in the dining area came on and a peppy Dean Martin melody filled the air. The pleasant song had the older patrons smiling and some clapping to the music. A buzz of chatter filled the room as diners looked around with curiosity.

The sound of a knife clinking on a water glass quieted the room. Then the music stopped as if on cue.

"What's going on?" His grandfather turned in his seat and looked around.

"Over there, by the window, Gramps." Sam had spotted Anthony Moretti seated with Eleanor a few minutes ago and realized exactly what was happening.

"That's Olivia's father," Gus whispered. "And Eleanor Pickett."

"Sure is." Liv's father hadn't shared the details of his surprise proposal, but apparently tonight was the night.

Anthony turned and faced the other patrons. "My apologies for interrupting everyone's dinner. I'd like you to be my witnesses tonight." He began to kneel and then shook his head. "You'll excuse me if I don't get down on one knee, but I'm not sure I could get up again without calling the paramedics."

A titter of laughter rang out.

Instead of kneeling, Anthony moved to stand next to Eleanor. Love beamed on her face.

"Eleanor, I never thought that I would be blessed to find true love twice in my lifetime, but I have. I love you, sweet lady. I may not be a young man anymore, but I still have all my parts, though the warranty has run out on most."

More laughter echoed through the dining room.

He pulled a small black box from his jacket pocket and opened the lid, offering the contents to her. "Will you do me the honor of becoming my wife?"

Sam was once again reminded of another ring. Another proposal. He looked away for a moment, indulging himself in the what-ifs that he normally ignored.

What if Liv had stuck around?

What if I'd gone after her?

"Oh, Anthony. Yes, of course. I love you." Eleanor held out her hand as the restaurant patrons swooned aloud and then applauded.

"Well, what do you know?" Gramps said. He stood and clapped his hands together.

"That's enough to make me go all teary-eyed. Good for them."

"He asked me to be his best man," Sam said.

Gus sat down. "You're pretty good at keeping secrets, aren't you?"

"I guess so. This has been in the works since Father's Day. I'm glad for him."

Liv walked past, and he called her name.

She sniffed and turned away, hiding her face. "I'll be with you shortly, Sam. I need some air."

Sam's heart tightened. This couldn't be easy for Liv, and he was concerned.

"Gramps, I'm going to check on her. She looked a little upset."

He walked down the hall past the kitchen, where wafts of delicious aromas spilled into the hallway and staff called out orders and spoke to each other in their own kitchen language.

"Did the chicken temp out?"

"Corner!"

"Put that in on the fly, please!"

Sam heard voices on the patio. He turned

to walk away, then stopped when voices drifted to him.

"Are you okay?" Robyn asked.

"Yes. I'm being silly. It was so sweet and so romantic. It had me thinking about..." Liv paused. "Never mind. I have to get back. My father will be looking for me."

The door opened, and Sam couldn't get out of the way fast enough. Liv nearly ran into him and he put his hands on her shoulders to prevent a collision.

"Oh, Sam, sorry." She looked up, her eyes moist.

"Liv? Are you all right?"

"Yes. I'm fine. I had a moment there. So much is going on. So many memories."

"Yeah. I get that." He nodded. "If you need to talk, I'm here."

"Thank you." She slipped her arms around his waist and hugged him.

Sam stood frozen and stunned by the gesture. Her soft hair tickled his chin.

"You're a good friend," she murmured before releasing him.

Yep, that's what he was—a good friend.

Something had changed though and being her good friend was no longer enough.

He couldn't keep denying his feelings for Liv. Yeah, he had a lot think to about.

Sam returned to his table, and moments later, Liv appeared with the waitstaff and an oversize cupcake with a candle.

"For me?" Gus asked. His eyes sparkled with delight, and his ears turned red as the staff sang "Happy Birthday."

The flame of the single candle on the cupcake glowed. Sam kept his attention on its swaying dance instead of looking up at Liv. Soon she and the waiters left them to their dessert.

"You sure you don't want some of this cupcake, Sam? It's more than I can eat after that meal." Gus sat back in his chair. "How'd she know I like chocolate? That Olivia is amazing."

"Yeah, she is."

"What are you thinking about so hard?" Gramps asked.

"I'm taking it all in so I remember this night."

"This has been a night to remember,

hasn't it?" Gramps said with a grin. "Pretty girls sang happy birthday to me, and I got to sit in on a romantic proposal. Not every day you see true love. If I wait around for you boys, I'll be waiting forever."

"What about Drew? He's the poster boy for true love."

"Well, here's a secret. I had a hand in that. Hammered Drew until he finally did what I told him. He let Sadie know he loved her."

Sam processed that bit of information as his grandfather kept talking.

"I've always thought you were the smartest of the bunch. You've been a mathematical genius for as long as I can remember."

Uh-oh, here it came. The compliment before the takedown. Sam braced himself.

"We're coming on the Fourth of July this weekend. Olivia has been back in town for two months now. How long are you going to wait before you make a move?"

"You seem certain she wants me to make a move."

"I've seen the way she looks at you when

you aren't noticing. Like a few minutes ago when she brought out that cupcake."

Sam scoffed at the words.

"Must be something in the drinking water at Lazy M. I'll look into a filtration system," Gus said.

"That's it," Sam joked. "No more Dr. Pepper. You're not making any sense."

"Sure I am. The way I figure it, you and your brothers are drinking something that made you all grow up scared about falling in love."

"Not true. I fell in love once. You know how that turned out. I was humiliated when she left town."

His grandfather's face grew serious. "Son, you're still in love. And you're terrified."

"Only a fool gets back on an unbroken horse, Gramps." His grandfather might be right, but that didn't mean he ought to act on his feelings.

"I hate to point out the obvious," his grandfather continued. "And I'm not calling you out, but you were a bronc rider once. A losing proposition in my mind, though no one asked me. You knew the odds when you got on that horse, yet you still did it. Same thing applies to relationships."

"If only it were that simple." His grandfather romanticized the world. Life wasn't romantic. It was messy and complicated. Which was why he put his faith in God, not people.

His grandfather looked at him hard. "You're overthinking this."

"I'm going to need a little time to overthink what you just said, Gramps."

Gramps started laughing. A deep belly laugh that had people turning to look.

That got Sam laughing. And why not? The situation was comical at best. He was right back where he'd started. In love with a woman who was going to break his heart.

What was he going to do about it? That was the real question.

"Busy again." Liv stared at her phone. She'd tried to reach Sam three times since he'd been at the restaurant with Gus last Wednesday. His phone was either busy or went to voice mail. She'd gotten a few thumbs-ups when she sent texts, so she knew he was still kicking.

He'd even cancelled dinner with her father on Sunday. That wasn't like Sam. Maybe he was sick. She'd happily bring him meatball soup, except she didn't even have directions to his house. Somewhere on the Lazy M Ranch. Perhaps she should call Gus and see if he was okay.

Liv flipped through her digital calendar. Here it was Monday, and she planned to spend the morning in The Inspired Kitchen reviewing the financials. Except she couldn't find this week's accounting paperwork from Sam.

"Miss Olivia, did you put these boxes in the storage room? I don't remember seeing them when I locked up on Saturday evening."

Liv followed Jane to the back room. Five cartons of Sam's woodcrafts sat against the wall, with inventories taped to the top. She stared at the boxes, searching for a plausible response to how they had gotten there. It was apparent Sam had dropped them off. But when?

"Oh yes," Liv improvised. "More supplies from our craftsman. They were dropped off yesterday." Or maybe it was Saturday night that the ninja craftsman stopped by. There was no way of knowing for certain.

"Do you want me to take care of them this morning?"

"If you don't mind. I can watch the front while you do that."

"Surely, I can. I'll make this my top priority."

"Thanks, Jane."

Liv stood at the counter, thinking. What could she have done to distance Sam?

Was he mad?

Perhaps it wasn't her. Maybe he was getting nervous because her father had asked him to be his best man. She recalled his panic when he thought Anthony wanted to talk weddings on Father's Day. Goodness, he'd probably thought her father was going to railroad him into proposing to his daughter again. That would be an excellent reason to avoid her.

Yes, that made sense. After all, the last time she'd seen him was when her father proposed at the restaurant. That evening had made her sentimental. No doubt it had affected Sam as well, bringing back painful memories of her departure.

She released a breath.

Or maybe he was upset about the store. His crafts were doing well, and so was the other merchandise. Could it be that she was outselling him, and he didn't want her to know? No, Sam was not a petty person. And if he was ahead in the challenge, why wasn't he doing an I-told-you-so dance?

The entire situation was suspect.

The chimes on the front door began to sing as Mindy Ellwood stepped into the shop.

"It's like a sauna out there." She fanned herself with a hand and then looked up at Liv. "Don't you look adorbs," she gushed. "Where did you get that cute sundress?"

Liv looked down at her outfit. She barely remembered what she'd put on this morning. "I don't remember where I got it, to tell you the truth."

"Well, it's cute. Oh, and congratulations," she continued. "Everyone is talking about that proposal. Your father is such a romantic."

"He really is," Liv agreed.

"If you need a dress for the wedding, I just got a shipment of the sweetest pastels. They say pastels are going to be big this fall." Mindy walked through the shop, glancing at the merchandise. She examined a stack of nestled sherbet-colored mixing bowls. Then she picked up the matching silicon spatulas. They were available in strawberry, peach, lemon and lime colors. But Mindy didn't take them to the register with her. Why not? She herself said pastels were going to be hot.

Liv needed to look into the psychology behind customer-purchase habits.

"How can I help you?" Liv asked when Mindy finally made it to the front counter.

"I'm here to chat woman-to-woman." Today her earrings were pink hoops, and they swayed when she moved her head.

"Okay. What does that mean?" Liv asked.

Mindy eyed Liv. "I've run the optics on the available men in this town. The Morgan boys are the most eligible bachelors.

Sadly, Drew is taken. Trevor is in hiding, and Lucas is never around. That puts a target on Sam, and you've done the impossible and snagged him." She shrugged. "I thought you could give me some dating tips."

Liv frowned. Where did this woman get her intel?

"Mindy, I'm as single as you are. I haven't had a date in over a year."

She stared at the blonde. Clearly, Liv was going to have to exercise her newfound boundary-setting skills here.

"I'm terribly busy. Monday is the only day I get to spend the entire day in the shop."

"Then, let's schedule a girls' night out. I'm trying to figure out why the fellas run when they see me coming."

Was Mindy ready to hear that her approach was a bit aggressive? She was scaring the single men.

"What makes you think I have advice?" Liv asked.

"Because you're doing something right, honey. I have a straight view from my cash register to the Snodgrass Building. Sam Morgan walks by your restaurant at least once a week and takes a peek."

"He does?"

"Yes." There was a long pause as Mindy's eyes rounded. She blinked, alarm on her face. "Maybe he's stalking you."

"Or maybe he's hungry. We post the weekly menu outside, you know." Liv frowned. "When was the last time you saw him?"

"Yesterday. This time, he was driving. He slowed his truck as he drove by and looked right into your store."

Liv straightened at the words. "Sunday? Is your shop even open on Sunday?"

"Not usually. But it's almost July, so I was doing inventory yesterday. I want to be ready for the Fourth of July crowd."

Sam had canceled dinner with her father so he could sneak inventory into the store when he knew she wouldn't be around. She couldn't very well tell Mindy that, or it would reveal the identity of the craftsman and destroy any chance she had of winning the challenge. Once the town folks found out Sam was the crafter, they'd knock down the doors to support him.

Liv was determined to win that challenge, and she wouldn't give up the shop before her lease was up.

"He's my landlord," Liv replied. "Maybe he saw a light bulb out, or maybe the security alarm was acting up. He isn't stalking me."

"I hope you're right. He looks harmless enough, but you never know. They say serial killers always look like the guy next door."

Liv tried not to laugh at the suggestion that Sam was a serial killer. Mindy had the best of intentions. To her credit, she'd tried multiple times to be social. Maybe Liv ought to give the woman a chance. She was new to town, and Liv sort of was too.

If she was really in Homestead Pass for the long haul, she could use a few more friends.

"Mindy, I'm a chef. My nights are booked. But I can do lunch. Are you free today? Would you care to join me at the restaurant?"

"It isn't open on Mondays. I looked."

"It's always open for me." Liv smiled. "I've got a baked ziti in the fridge that I could warm up. We can have it with a pear-and-Gorgonzola salad and fresh bread. Maybe cheesecake for dessert?"

"Or I can eat a peanut-butter-and-jelly sandwich at my desk." Mindy laughed. "What time? And I'll definitely bring my own doggie bag."

This time, Liv laughed. "Noon?"

"I'll be there. Oh, and thank you for special ordering those cutting boards. I'm incredibly pleased with them." She glanced around again. "Everyone is talking about those mini hope chests. Any chance you have one in stock?"

"I have a delivery that hasn't been unpacked. How about if I let you know at lunchtime?"

"That works."

"See you then," Mindy said. She began to turn away and then turned back. "No wonder Sam likes you."

"I, ah… Thank you."

As Mindy exited, Liv stared after her for

a moment, then tried to remember what she'd been doing before the interruption.

Financials! She stepped into the storage room, where her manager was buried in a pile of packing paper. "Jane, how are the woodcraft product numbers? Any idea?"

"Oh yes. I keep the information on a spreadsheet since it's a consignment, and I can tell you they are doing very well."

"Better than the rest of the merchandise?"

"I don't know that, but I suppose I could figure it out. You've got that fancy software program on the computer. Except I don't have the password to access it."

"Who has that?"

"Mr. Morgan."

Sam. Of course. "Thanks, Jane. I'll see if I can get that password."

Surely Sam wasn't doing better than she was.

Liv mulled things over for a few minutes and then began to stroll around the store, assessing the merchandise with a critical eye. The cookbooks were doing well. She'd even had to put in a second order on them.

It turned out everyone in Homestead Pass wanted to be the next award-winning home chef.

Maybe she should write a cookbook. But that wouldn't solve the problem here and now. If she wanted to sell pots, pans and utensils, she'd have to show her customers why they needed them.

Store demos. That was the solution. Liv perked up at the idea. Once they saw the amazing confections that she whipped up using the products, they'd be fighting over those bowls.

Yes! She'd start cooking demonstrations in the store using an electric stove top. All she'd need would be a table and a dozen chairs for her audience. It would be a free, ticketed event. Limited seating. Not everyone could attend. They'd have to register.

Liv pulled out her phone and searched for party rentals.

There was no way that she was going to let Sam win this challenge. If he thought he was going to run her out of Homestead Pass he was wrong. It was time to up her game.

Chapter Eleven

Liv strolled through the restaurant dining room to the front window, admiring the table decor on the way. It might be cheesy, but she loved the variety of red-white-and-blue linens and the single white rosebud on each table to create a patriotic theme.

"Lots of traffic today," she called to Loretta in the kitchen. "Every parking spot is taken. Steve is giving out tickets for parking in front of the fire hydrant."

"Fourth of July weekend," Loretta said. "It's always busy."

Liv lifted the shade on the front door for a better look and did a double take. "No. Something is going on out there. That's not the usual holiday traffic. Maybe the grocer is having another one of his buy-one, get-one sales on watermelon." She stopped at the hostess stand and checked the computer reservation system. "The seating is completely booked. Nothing available for walk-ins."

Liv strolled back to the kitchen, where her aunt kneaded bread on the prep table with an ease that Liv envied. "Which is why I'm making extra loaves."

"Do you think we should outsource the bread?" Liv asked.

"No. It's become our trademark. I've heard comments numerous times suggesting that no one makes Italian loaves like we do. We need more of that kind of publicity."

"Thank you for your recipe, Nonna," she murmured.

"Is that your phone, Olivia?" Loretta Moretti looked around the kitchen.

"Yes." Liv reached for her purse and pulled out her cell. She'd missed a call from Jane at The Inspired Kitchen. The store manager handled everything with an efficiency that scared Liv. It had to be important if Jane called.

"Zia, I'm going next door for a moment."

"Take your time. I'm not going anywhere soon."

"If you have to leave before I get back, just lock up. I have my key."

"Sounds good. Oh, and Olivia, didn't you have your first cooking demonstration this morning? How did that go?"

Liv grinned. "Unbelievable. I should have done this sooner. I drove to a printer in Elk City on Monday and had a standup banner of myself holding a spatula and mixing bowl made. Jane and I created a small area for demos."

"Very good," Loretta said with a nod.

"It was a huge success. Thirty people registered." Excited, Liv gestured with her hands. She'd been thrilled when the ticketed event had booked up so quickly. "Maybe because it's a Saturday and the Fourth of July weekend. Or maybe because of the free samples of lemon icebox pie." She shrugged. "I'm not sure which, but we totally sold out of the large mixing bowls and the spatula I used in the demonstration."

Loretta beamed. "Wow! That's wonderful."

"Yes. I'm already thinking about the next one."

Liv grabbed a bakery box full of pastel macarons from the counter. "These are another marketing ploy. Let's see if I can sell out of the silicon baking mats I use to create the macarons." She plucked her keys from the hook near the kitchen entrance.

"So, you're pleased with your venture so far?" her aunt asked.

Liv walked farther into the kitchen. "I am... We both know there are no guarantees in this business. My plan is to review the restaurant financials in the fall to determine our bottom line. Papà and Eleanor are getting married in late October, and I'm not thinking any further ahead than that. This is my dream, Zia, and I'm happy here."

Loretta stopped kneading for a moment. "I'm glad to hear this... Have you spoken to Sam about the future?"

"Sam?"

"The man is at the house all the time. I can't help but think that he's got a vested interest in your future as well."

Liv blinked, surprised at her aunt's words. "He popped in twice after Papà was discharged. It wasn't for me."

Loretta laughed. "Yes, my dearest, he's there for you. And you missed the time he stopped by and you were in Elk City shopping for supplies."

"Really?" She pondered the words. "He certainly hasn't acted like that's the case lately. I can't get him to answer his phone. You noticed that he bailed on Sunday dinner?"

"Men are funny. They spook easily." She looked pointedly at Liv.

"That was the past, Zia. Things have changed. For one, I'm no longer pressured by my father. I make my own decisions—and I've decided to stay here."

"Maybe you should tell Sam that."

"I have."

"Tell him again." She smiled. "I want you to be happy, and I can't help but think

Sam Morgan might be part of the equation."

"I'll have to think on that." Liv gave her aunt a kiss on the cheek. *"Ti voglio bene a tua, Zia."*

"I love you, too, Olivia."

Liv walked from the restaurant's courtyard, along the brick path, to the back door of the shop, her steps determined as she considered her aunt's words. Liv had survived a tornado and Sam Morgan's opposition. No, she wasn't going to run ever again.

But was it coincidence that he'd gone to ground since her father's proposal? Were they back to square one?

She unlocked the door and slipped inside. "Jane? You called me?"

The back room was eerily quiet. Liv noticed the storeroom was open. She stepped in. Sam's inventory was kept on the left side. The neat stacks were double-checked by Jane when they came in and stored in an orderly manner. Except the boxes were overturned with packing paper strewn all over. "What is this?" she murmured.

She crossed the room to get a closer look. Every box was empty. He'd dropped off five boxes on Monday. Could all the merchandise be on the shelves?

Liv stepped into the front of the store and stopped. The place was packed. Wall-to-wall shoppers. Notably all women.

The fifty-dollar ad that she'd placed in the *Homestead Pass Daily Journal* had paid off. This was good. Excessive, but good.

One of the part-time college girls Liv had hired stood at the counter ringing up sales, while another carefully wrapped a cutting board in white packing paper. Both looked harried. A conga line of customers snaked from the register to the front door.

Liv slid the tray of macarons on the counter behind the register and righted the banner with her smiling image, which had somehow ended up on the floor. She did her best to wipe the footprint off her face.

The buzz of excitement in the room had Liv smiling. Customers were bumping into each other as they moved up and down the aisles with their arms full of merchandise.

Note to self—purchase hand baskets. It made sense to make it easy for customers to shop to their heart's content.

"Sherry, are all these people here for the Fourth of July sale?" Liv whispered to the girl manning the wrapping station.

"Not exactly." Sherry blew her bangs out of her face and shot Liv a look of confusion.

"Not exactly?"

"They're all here to buy woodcrafts."

"All of them?"

"Uh-huh." Sherry continued to wrap as she spoke.

Liv looked around. "I don't recognize any of these women."

"They all came over from Elk City."

"Elk City," Liv murmured, excitement growing. The newspaper article must have come through. Excellent. The article was already bringing in out-of-towners. She looked around again. This was more than she'd expected. Still, this kind of publicity was what she recommended to her clients and Liv was thrilled to see it work so well for her own business.

"Have you seen Mrs. Smith?" Liv asked.

"Over there, next to Sam's stuff. She had to break up an argument. It almost ended in fisticuffs. Two women wanted the last hope chest."

Liv started walking and stopped. She whirled around. "Wait. Did you say Sam's stuff?"

"Oh, so I'm sorry, Ms. Moretti. Mr. Morgan's stuff."

A cold dread trickled through Liv. "How did you know he's the crafter?"

Sherry pointed to a copy of the *Elk City Daily News* on the counter. "That article about you came out today. Except it's about Mr. Morgan."

Liv gasped at the color photo of Sam Morgan on the front page.

Local bronc buster is also an award-winning woodcrafter.

"You've got to be kidding me." Liv picked up the paper for a closer look. It was Sam all right, though the picture was from his rodeo days. The photo caught Sam's best assets—the sparkling blue eyes, the Morgan smile and his trophy buckle. The picture reminded her of Lucas. Like his brother, Sam had been a cowboy charmer not very long ago, and this picture was enough to make any woman swoon.

Surely Sam hadn't done this. Liv fought the urge to jump to conclusions.

Hadn't they been getting closer each day? She thought maybe she was falling in love with him again. Was that part of his plan too?

Get her to fall in love with him and then pull the rug out from under her? It seemed to be working.

Jane stepped up to the counter. She released a breath and leaned against it. "This place has been slammed since the Elk City paper came out. I didn't make the connection until one of our customers pointed it out."

Liv skimmed the article. It was a detailed write-up that painted a nice picture of the Lazy M Ranch and Sam's rodeo days and detailed his woodworking.

"Is the restaurant mentioned at all?" Liv asked.

"Page ten," Jane said with a grimace.

Liv flipped through the pages, haphazardly, until she got to a small grainy picture of the exterior of Moretti's Farm-to-Table Bistro. The accompanying article was nice, but no one would be banging on her door to get in, courtesy of this article. Disappointment wrapped itself around her.

She'd offered the reporter and photographer her best double-chocolate biscotti for nothing. Liv took a deep breath and fought the urge to shred the paper into tiny pieces.

Fine. It's all fine. The restaurant stood on its own merits.

"We're almost out of Mr. Morgan's inventory," Jane said. "It would be advisable to let him know." The manager eyed her and frowned. "I know it's not my place to ask, but was there a reason Mr. Morgan chose to keep his identity confidential until now?"

"There are a few reasons," Liv hedged.

She shook her head in dismay. The bargain they'd agreed upon was the primary reason. Because Sam wanted to make their agreement fair.

A small crash had both Jane and Liv turning. A young woman in a pink cowboy hat, a fringed Western shirt and matching chaps scooped up a cutting board from the floor. "Oops. So sorry."

Liv blinked. She hadn't even considered that every buckle bunny within the radius of a copy of the *Elk City Daily News* was about to descend upon the store. Was it possible they were already here? Liv started counting heads and gave up.

Why now? Why had Sam chosen to let the cat out of the bag now? They'd had a solid agreement in place. This broke the challenge rules. Maybe he was tired of waiting to get his store back.

Was that why he'd distanced himself of late?

Liv didn't know what to think. She reached for a macaron and shoved it in her mouth. Could things possibly get worse?

The bells on the front door chimed, and

in walked Mindy, looking peeved. She took one glance around and strode past the line, straight to the register.

"I can't believe you were holding out on me after our cheesecake bonding. Sam Morgan is your secret weapon. That's why he kept coming around."

Liv sighed. "Do you get the Elk City paper too?"

"No. One of my customers told me about the article."

"I told you we weren't dating, didn't I?" Liv picked up the tray and held it out as a peace offering. "Macaron?"

"Ooh, thanks." Mindy grabbed a handful and glanced around the store with a critical eye. "Why was it such a big secret?"

"Why does everyone keep asking me that?" Liv shook her head. "It was Sam's idea. Not mine."

"This place is out of control. Sam needs his own store," Mindy said. "He doesn't have enough real estate in here with the other stuff."

"The other stuff is why I opened this store," Liv said.

Mindy tilted her head. "Maybe you need to rethink that. If the customer wants Sam, you should give them Sam. You can't hold on to what isn't working."

"I've only been open a month." She put down the macarons in her hand and rubbed the bridge of her nose. "I don't know if it's working or not."

"Olivia, it's pretty obvious. I mean, you can see that this *is* working, right?"

Liv looked around. It was difficult to be objective when she was so annoyed.

"Did you know that article was coming out?" Mindy asked.

"Yes, but it was supposed to be about *me*. If I'd had a heads-up, I might have been prepared." Although, there was probably no way to prepare for this crowd.

"Sam should be down here, talking to his fans. The man could sell his grocery list or even these." Mindy reached for a pair of kitschy potholders embroidered with red lips. "Why isn't he here helping you sell the other merch?" She narrowed her eyes.

"He might not be a serial killer, but he's taking advantage of your good nature."

Mindy was right about that. He'd caused this problem, and he ought to be here to deal with it. Liv pulled out her phone and punched in his number. As usual, he didn't pick up.

Maybe a follow-up text would help.

SOS. Emergency at store. Need help ASAP.

Jane rushed back up to the register. The normally calm manager appeared to be on her last nerve. "People are asking if they can put orders in for items we're out of. I know that hasn't been our practice in the past, but if we don't, I fear this crowd may revolt."

"Mr. Morgan's items, I presume," Liv said.

Jane nodded.

Sam would be furious if they did that.

"Yes, Jane. Let's take orders," Liv said. Later, she'd pray for forgiveness for smiling as she said it.

* * *

Sam took off his work gloves and reached for the water bottle he'd placed on top of the stall. He needed time away from people. Normally, that would happen on his porch at dusk. But it was too hot, and the skeeters were too hungry. So he had headed to the stables to feed the horses and muck stalls. No one ever wanted the job, but today, horses were preferable to people. And the stables had huge circulating fans to keep the air moving.

"You left your phone in the main house, right next to the cinnamon rolls."

Sam turned at Trevor's voice. "Thanks." The cell buzzed as he took it from his brother.

"I couldn't help but notice the text was from Olivia. Looks important," Trevor said.

"Does it?" He read Liv's message, shoved the phone into his pocket and returned to the task at hand.

"Aren't you going to head downtown?"

"Does it look like I'm going some-where?" Sam asked.

"That text said it was an emergency."

"It's a home goods store. What kind of emergency could it be?"

"You want me to check it out?" Trevor asked. "I'm happy to go, and I smell a lot better than you do."

Sam groaned. He was the landlord and he should go. After all, he was obligated to take care of things through the week, after which, he'd announce that he had officially won the bargain.

He took zero pleasure in the fact. This mess was all his fault.

It was also his fault he found himself in love with Liv again.

"Sam?" Trevor peered at him. "I said I'll go."

"Not necessary. I'll go after I take a quick shower."

"You sure? I'm happy to run down there for you."

"I said I'm going."

"You okay?" Trevor asked. "You've been awful cranky. And what are you doing in here anyhow?"

"That's got to be the dumbest question

I've heard all day." Sam slowly turned around, eyeing his brother. "What does it look like I'm doing?"

Trevor inhaled sharply. "Last time you were this cranky was when Olivia left. I had hoped we wouldn't revisit those days again." His brother pulled off his hat, slapped it against his thigh and put it back on. "I knew nothing good would come of her being back."

"I'm not cranky," Sam said. "And Liv hasn't done anything. This is one hundred percent my own doing. Got it?"

Trevor raised his gloved hands and backed up. "Yeah, I got it."

Sam stalked out of the stables to grab a shower and find out what this so-called emergency was.

The shower calmed him some, as did the praise-and-worship music blaring from his speakers on his way into town. It was difficult to be down when he was getting into the thankful zone. And he had much to be thankful for.

Parking wasn't one of those things.

"What is going on in this town?" He

said the words aloud after his third time circling the block. Finally, he pulled into a primo space in front of Mindy's boutique. The blonde opened the door of her shop and glared at him before shutting the door and turning over the welcome sign to Closed.

Sam looked from Glitz & Glam to the Snodgrass Building. He didn't have a good feeling about this.

The sign on The Inspired Kitchen said they were closed as well. Sam checked his watch. It had taken him a while to get here, but it was only 4:00 p.m. The store didn't normally close until six. He walked around back and let himself in.

Walking down the hall to the front of the shop, the first thing he saw was Liv sitting on a chair with her feet up, eating macarons.

"Shouldn't you be at the restaurant?"

"Thanks for showing up so fast. Did you break the sound barrier on the way over?"

Sam jerked back at her sharp tone.

"Sorry. I, ah, was working." He looked around. Besides Liv's obvious dour mood, something was off in the shop, but he couldn't quite put his finger on the issue.

"What's the emergency?"

"Do you see any *SJ*-crafted pieces?"

Sam blinked. The shelves that usually displayed his merchandise were empty.

"You were robbed! Did you call Steve and file a report?" He walked over to the alarm panel. "I didn't get a notification from the security company."

"It didn't go off."

His heart began to pound. "You were robbed in broad daylight? Are you all right? Was anyone hurt?" He looked around again. "Where is everyone?"

"I sent them home. They were exhausted."

"Okay...good. No one was hurt. People are more important than things. Do you have insurance coverage?"

"Yes. Of course, I have insurance, but we weren't robbed." Liv dropped her feet to the ground with a thud, stood and handed him a newspaper. "My interview came out today. Except it's *your* interview."

Sam's jaw sagged. It was hard to miss his picture on the front page. Who'd given the press that picture? He skimmed the article. It was flattering, but much of the substance stretched the truth a bit.

Then he turned the pages to find a small picture of Liv's restaurant and a write-up. He grimaced.

"How did this happen?" he asked.

Liv cocked her head and looked at him. "You tell me."

Why was she asking him? "I didn't have anything to do with this."

"How did they get that picture?"

Sam's mind raced, searching for an answer. There wasn't one. "I don't know."

"Why didn't you tell me you were an award-winning craftsman?"

Award-winning craftsman? And just like that, everything became clear. The only award he'd ever won for his woodworking was in junior high. A dead giveaway as to who'd leaked this information to the press.

None other than his grandpa, Augustus Morgan.

"Um… I don't like to brag," Sam said.

"Your identity was supposed to remain secret," Liv said, her voice becoming tight and ominous. "It's safe to assume that you won our challenge. Even if you failed to abide by the rules."

"Liv, I didn't have anything to do with this."

Yep, it had to be Gramps, but he wasn't going to throw the man under the bus.

"You have it all wrong," Sam said.

"Do I? Was all this about payback?" Her brown eyes were raw with pain. "Are we even now?"

Hurting Liv was a kick in the gut. Sam took a deep breath. "You've got this all wrong."

"Do I? I thought that our partnership was based on trust. Now it's clear you still don't trust me."

"Trust." He mulled the word over. "Yeah, trust is a tricky thing. Isn't it? Trust is supposed to be a two-way street, and you clearly don't trust me if you really think I could have done this."

Liv put her hands on her hips and stared him down. "All I know is that we have an agreement. I intend to stick to the rules. We aren't done with this challenge for another week, so I suggest you plan accordingly."

The hair on his neck stood up at her words. "Plan accordingly?"

"That newspaper article brought in over one hundred women in four hours, all looking for Sam Morgan crafts. It could have been more, but I lost count after they knocked down my banner half a dozen times. They cleaned us out."

"Everything?"

"Everything." She shrugged. "Since you failed to maintain inventory as agreed, we've been forced to take orders. I'll provide you with the special-order list. It's quite extensive."

He couldn't believe what he was hearing. Special orders. He'd be buried for weeks.

"You weren't supposed to do that, Liv. When am I going to find time for special orders? I have a day job. Counting this job, I have three jobs."

"Maybe you need to have a serious conversation with yourself about your plans for the future." She crossed her arms. "And maybe you should start reevaluating your priorities. I thought you were a man of your word. I'm so disappointed in you."

Sam turned and walked out without another word.

Yeah, maybe he should start reevaluating his priorities. He should have never made a bargain with a woman who held the power to break his heart. Again.

Chapter Twelve

"Are you telling me Sam won?" Liv asked. She flipped through the papers Jane had put on her desk and looked up.

"Won?" Jane cocked her head, perplexed. "I'm sorry. I don't understand the question. Won what?"

"Didn't you just say that Sam's wood-crafts were outselling every other product in the shop before that newspaper article came out?"

"Yes, ma'am. Mr. Morgan gave me all the accounting paperwork and the pass-word to the bookkeeping program when he dropped off the inventory this morn-ing. I reviewed everything. It's right there on that spreadsheet I printed out for you."

"Unbelievable," Liv murmured. He'd been winning from day one and hadn't told her.

"Was there anything else, Miss Olivia?"

"No. Thank you. I appreciate your hard work, Jane."

"Thank you." She paused. "Did I do something wrong?"

"What? No. Not at all."

"You seem upset, so I thought maybe I caused a problem."

"No. You're wonderful, Jane." Liv offered a reassuring smile. "I'm fortunate to have you. You certainly have not caused a problem." *It's Sam who's caused the problem.*

"Thank you. I can tell you I love my job. The hours are perfect too. I can still attend Wednesday evening church and babysit my grandbaby on Sunday."

"I'm glad it's working out for you."

"If there's nothing else, I'll unpack those boxes Mr. Morgan left."

"Sounds like a plan."

Liv tried not to think about Sam's abrupt visit to the store this morning. He'd stacked the boxes in the supply room and talked to Jane, ignoring her. Not even a good morning or an apology for leaking the information to the news. The rebuff hurt.

After all these weeks, Liv had come to depend on Sam and enjoy his company more than she could have ever expected when she began this journey back in May. She found herself looking up when the door to the shop or the restaurant opened, hoping he'd appear.

Though everything was out of control, Liv was calm-headed today. She regretted her outburst with Sam. The truth was she shouldered at least half the blame for yesterday's fiasco.

She had been so preoccupied with the restaurant that she hadn't hounded Sam for the numbers as she should have. When he'd said that her merchandise had been moving well, Liv assumed that meant she was outselling him. She hadn't even questioned him because she wanted to believe her merchandise was hot. It wasn't. Sales of her products had improved when she began the in-store demonstrations, but they weren't close to Sam's numbers.

She looked at the spreadsheet again, but she still couldn't wrap her head around the facts. Sam had been winning all along.

From the beginning, she'd only been concerned with what she wanted. The shop. So she'd gone on defense and hadn't looked at things from Sam's point of view.

The realization had her grimacing. She should have never agreed to the bargain and never agreed to keep his crafts anonymous. By acquiescing, she hadn't respected his goals any more than her father respected hers. She should have encouraged him to make it known that he was the crafter. He ought to have had the opportunity to take pride in his work.

On the other hand, Sam wasn't exactly innocent. Liv rubbed her head when she realized she was back where she'd started with one slight difference. She'd allowed herself to fall in love with Sam again.

Why hadn't he told her he was going to reveal his identity to the press? She would have been onboard.

Nothing made any sense.

Liv picked up the *Elk City Daily News* from her desk and reread the article. It had only been twenty-four hours since the paper came out, and her world had been turned upside down. She yawned and reached for the cold remains of her coffee.

Last night had been a sleepless one. She'd paced the floor, trying to come up with a solution that might work for both her and Sam. Mindy's words kept coming back to her. *You can't hold on to what isn't working.* Mindy was right. The paperwork on Liv's desk proved it. The way she'd been operating was not working. Sam's crafts were the big attraction. His merchandise needed more space in the shop. The only way that could happen was if she conceded.

Liv was willing to give up the space but not her plans. She'd simply been going about this all wrong. The cooking demos proved that people were willing to buy mixing bowls, pots, pans and spatulas too, when they thought they could duplicate her recipes. They also loved her restaurant.

So why hadn't she put both winning scenarios together?

About 3:00 a.m., she'd also decided that Sam needed a little boot-to-the-backside encouragement to go after his dreams. Maybe if she helped him figure out what he wanted, things could go back to the way they had been.

Day by day, over the last two months, she'd worked at gaining his trust and forgiveness. Liv wasn't about to throw that away. She cared about Sam and wanted a chance to prove that to him. And if he wouldn't give her a chance, then at least this time, she'd walk away knowing she'd done her part to force him to wake up and grab his own personal brass ring.

She glanced at the clock and got up from her desk. Yes, it was time to turn the tables on her cowboy crafter. Tucking the newspaper in her purse, Liv went in search of her manager. She found Jane sitting on a stool in the storage room, removing wrapped merchandise from boxes with the care of a museum curator.

"Jane, I'll be back shortly."

"Yes, ma'am." She looked up at Liv. "Mind if I ask if everything is okay?"

"It is, but between you and me, things are about to change around here."

"Oh?"

"I'm moving the kitchenware part of the store in another direction."

"What direction is that?"

"Next door. Into the restaurant. Sam's merchandise needs more room in the shop. It makes sense logistically too. I won't have to keep running back and forth."

Jane's brow creased. "Will I be let go?"

"Not a chance. We need you. You'll stay right here."

"Wonderful." Jane smiled. "I imagine Mr. Morgan is excited about the expansion."

"Yes. Absolutely." *She hoped. First she had to tell him.*

Liv jumped into her pickup, jacked up the air and headed for the office of the *Homestead Pass Daily Journal.*

She opened the front door of the news office, ignored the protesting receptionist and strode straight into the office of the cranky editor she'd run into at the business association meeting. "Have you read this yet?" Liv placed the paper on his desk.

He raised his bushy white brows and shot her a bored glance before turning his attention back to his computer monitor. "What can I help you with?"

"The paper sold out in half a day. Wouldn't it be nice if your papers went that fast?"

"That so?" He picked up the newspaper, rustling the pages as he examined the article.

"Why is it you haven't jumped on this and gotten an interview with Sam?" Liv asked.

"You're in here too. Right there on page ten," he said.

"I'm an afterthought. Sam Morgan is the feature. Besides, I don't need the publicity, but I think Sam deserves some. I understand he does your books, as well as a dozen other small businesses in this town. I'm guessing he doesn't charge anything near what he should."

The editor's chair creaked as he leaned back and eyed Liv. "I've got a story on that gang of wild turkeys out on Milo Lane for the front page, ready to go to press. Color photo and everything."

"Wild turkeys?" Liv blinked. "Do you want to sell papers or not?"

"I suppose I could call Elk City and get permission to reprint their story." He looked her up and down. "You're kind of gutsy coming in here, considering you're the gal who dumped him."

"That, my friend, is old news."

Liv turned on her heel and left.

Sam saw Drew's lips moving but couldn't hear a thing his brother was saying. He turned off the planer and removed his mask, goggles and hearing protection. "What did you say?"

"I got your message." Drew glanced around the workshop. He inspected a stack of signs Sam had recently completed. Made of reclaimed barn wood, they'd been washed with an acrylic milk paint, giving them an old-world finish. Each sign had a different quote on the surface. The pieces were some of his bestsellers.

"Well, what do you know? Sadie put one of these up in our kitchen. I didn't realize you were the artist."

"Yeah, that's me. The man behind the inspirational quotes." The irony did not escape him. The cynical and beleaguered guy whose life was in the dumpster sold signs with uplifting messages for a living.

Drew ran a finger over the lettering. "How do you put those quotes on there?"

"Different techniques. Paint stencils, vinyl lettering or laser cuts."

"You're really good at this stuff, aren't you?"

"Try not to sound so surprised."

"I didn't mean to sound surprised, Sam." He paused. "Anyhow, you texted me. What did you need?"

Sam pointed to the boxes stacked near the door. "Can you drop these off in town? There's no rush, but they need to get there today."

"By town, you mean Olivia's shop?" Drew shook his head and gave a low whistle. "No can do."

"You don't have to talk to Liv. Just drop the boxes off. In. Out. Nobody gets hurt."

"If that's the case, then why don't you do it?" Drew shook his head. "I don't think so. My wife already warned me to stay out of your love life."

"My love life? I don't have a love life." Any hope of that disappeared with his last conversation with Liv. He looked at Drew. "And all I'm asking you to do is drop off boxes, not negotiate world peace."

"Word around town is something is going on. Did you see the Homestead Pass newspaper today?"

Sam closed his eyes and groaned. "Now what? I don't have time to read the paper."

"You ought to make time since you keep making the headlines. They reprinted the article from the *Elk City Daily News*. Everyone is talking." He frowned and crossed his arms. "I do believe my wife is right. I should stay out of it."

"You said everyone is talking. Specifically who is everyone?"

"All I know is that Mindy Ellwood talked to Sadie. The next thing I know, my wife's telling me to stay clear and mind my own business." He stepped toward the door. "This is me. Minding my own business."

Sam was fairly certain his blood pressure was about to hit an all-time high. He took a long slow breath. "Let me get this straight. You're refusing to help your own brother—your flesh and blood—move a few boxes, based on gossip Mindy told Sadie." He pinned his brother with his gaze. "Is that correct?"

Drew nodded. "Pretty much sums it up. I'm not getting myself in the doghouse because you've got women problems."

"*Woman*. Not *women*." Sam groaned. "There's only one woman who's giving me headaches."

"You do look kind of rough." Drew peered at Sam. "Are you losing sleep? Having focusing problems?"

"Yeah, how'd you know?"

"Had the same thing a year ago. Miserable. Absolutely miserable."

Maybe it was a virus or something. His throat did feel a little raw. "Did you go to the clinic?"

"No, unfortunately, I went to Gramps. I do not recommend that."

"What do you mean?"

"You're in love, pal."

Sam jerked to attention at the words. "I asked for a favor, not your misdiagnosis."

"I'm doing you a favor. I'm telling you to step up and drop the boxes off yourself."

Behind him, the door to the shop opened and Trevor and his grandfather walked in.

"Did we have a meeting scheduled?" Sam asked. "And close the door would you? That mini split is made to cool the shop, not the pasture."

Trevor's eyes rounded. He looked from Sam to Drew. "He bite your head off too?"

"Yeah." Drew nodded. "His attitude has deteriorated significantly since I arrived. I suggest you turn around and leave while you can."

"Ignore him. Was there something you need, Trev?" Sam asked. "Because if not, I have work to do."

"I brought Gramps here to tell you something."

Gramps shook his head, his expression sickly. "It's been my experience that timing is important in these delicate situations. I'll come back tomorrow."

"Whoa. Whoa. Whoa." Trevor jumped in front of the door. "No way, Gramps. We talked about this. You have to tell him."

Sam rubbed his jaw, confused. "Does someone want to tell me what's going on?"

"I did it," Gus said.

"What are you talking about, Gramps?" Sam asked.

"I told that Elk City newspaper lady that those were your pieces in Olivia's shop. I gave her the photo and told her about your award."

Sam had figured as much. "My award in junior high school. That was twenty-five years ago."

"That doesn't take away from the value of the award."

He warmed at his grandfather's words. "I see your point. Why did you talk to that reporter?" Sam asked.

"Bragging rights. I'm proud of you, son. We all are." He paused. "Also, I made a little trade with the woman. I promised her the inside scoop on the shop if she'd run a piece on the fishing derby."

Sam started laughing. The situation was so over-the-top, he had to laugh.

His brothers looked at each other, concern reflected in their eyes.

"That was very ingenious of you, Gramps," Sam said. "I already knew it was you, though."

"You did?" His grandfather released a breath. "Why didn't you say something?"

"It wasn't the end of the world. Someone would have figured it out eventually."

"I heard you sold out of everything because of the article," Gramps hedged.

"Yep. I've had to put my accounting and ranch chores on hold, trying to fill the orders the shop took. It's been a week with little sleep, but I've finished them."

Gus frowned and looked at Sam. "And I also heard that Olivia was fit to be tied."

"She'll get over it when those boxes are delivered." She wouldn't get over it, but that was another story for another day.

Gramps and Trevor looked at the stack of boxes.

"One of you want to drop them off for me?"

"No way," Trevor said, backing away from the inventory.

"Nope," Gramps added. "Telling you was tough enough. I'm not ready to admit my culpability in this particular crime."

Sam looked at Drew, and his brother raised his palms. "I didn't talk to them. But it doesn't take a genius to see a tornado on the horizon."

"On the other hand," Gramps said, "if you need an assistant in the workshop, I'm your guy. I'm fair to middling with a sander and I can paint like it's nobody's business."

Actually...that wasn't a bad idea, and it would mean he could spend more time with Gramps as well. "I could use an assistant," Sam admitted.

"I'll need a stool to sit on. I'm not as young as I used to be. Can't be standing all day."

"I have a stool and an apron."

"Then you got yourself an assistant."

"Great. We can start training on Monday. I'm taking Sunday off."

Trevor cut in. "Maybe you can find out what Liv's doing at the restaurant while you're in town."

"That's an excellent idea," Drew added. "She's doing some sort of renovation over there. I guess I should have mentioned that."

"Renovation?" Sam frowned. "What kind of renovation?" She hadn't discussed it with her landlord.

"The word is that there were fellas in white overalls going in there. They were carrying dry wall and paint buckets," Drew said.

"You better check it out. You're the landlord," Trevor said.

"We'll help you load the boxes so you can be on your way," Drew added.

Sam's gaze spanned the trio. They sure were in a rush to throw him to the wolves.

An hour later, he pulled up in front of The Inspired Kitchen with half a dozen reasons why this was a bad idea. He should have snuck the boxes into the shop after hours like the coward he was.

A tap at his window had him jumping. *Mindy.*

She was so petite that her head barely reached his window. He rolled it down, prepared for trouble, because the woman practically had smoke coming out of her ears.

"Are you stalking Liv again?" she demanded.

What? Sam looked at her, confused. He expected to her to read him the riot act. But stalking?

"I do not stalk," he said. The blonde glared with an intensity that had him inching away from the door.

"Then what are you doing, sitting in your truck, looking at the shop?"

"I'm trying to figure out if Liv is in there." He looked down at Mindy and frowned. "What are you? Her bodyguard?"

"I'm her friend and I'm watching out for her." She frowned. "She's at the restaurant. I saw her go in."

"Thanks."

"If you aren't stalking her, then what are you doing? Your behavior is highly suspicious."

"I have boxes to deliver." He sighed and shook his head. Life used to be a lot less complicated before he'd started bargaining with his ex-fiancée.

Mindy looked at him hard and then began to smile. "You're in love with her. Mrs. Pickett was right."

"No—"

Mindy raised a hand. "Please, I may be fun-sized, but I'm not dumb." She smiled again. "I'll be praying for you, Sam Morgan."

"Great. Just great." The grapevine was about to be reactivated. Sam got out of the truck and lowered the tailgate. He pulled out his hand truck and loaded the boxes.

In love. Both Drew and Mindy had accused him of the same thing. The whole thing was laughable. It didn't matter how he felt if he and Liv couldn't even make it through a summer without problems. How could he convince her to think about a future in Homestead Pass with him when she believed he'd sabotaged her?

He unlocked the back door of the shop and rolled the boxes in. The silver-haired manager greeted him with a welcoming smile. At least Jane liked him.

"Mr. Morgan. Am I glad to see you. I've had a few calls about those special orders."

He nodded. "I brought them with me. Everything is labeled. There's new merchandise as well."

"Wonderful."

Sam put the boxes in the storage room and turned to Jane. "Um, Mrs. Smith, do you know what's going on in the restaurant?"

She pursed her lips, considering the question. "I'm not at liberty to share that information. It's a secret. Miss Olivia was very clear about that."

He went back to the truck and brought in another load under Jane's watchful eye. When he'd carefully stacked the last of them on the left side, he handed her the inventory sheet.

"Thank you," she said.

"Are you sure you can't give me a hint?" he asked.

"I can tell you that I've committed to staying on here at the shop when Miss Olivia relocates." Her eyes popped wide. "Oh, my! I may have said too much already. Just know that I consider it an honor to work with you, Mr. Morgan."

Relocates? The word poleaxed him. Liv was leaving...again? After everything she'd done to try to win the shop, she wasn't sticking around?

He swallowed hard, working to respond to Jane. "I... Um... Thank you. I appreciate that. Commitment is hard to find these days."

There it was. History repeating itself. Sam wheeled the hand truck back to his vehicle and stared at the sky. Storm clouds hovered low in the distance. Maybe it would rain. He could use a good, cleansing rain before he decided what he was going to do about the ache in his chest that wouldn't go away.

* * *

Liv drove through the gates of the Lazy M Ranch with determination. She barely noticed the tall moss-covered stone pillars that stood guarding the entrance. No, her focus was on the final part of her plan.

Sam had declined her father's invitation to lunch again. Anthony was asking questions she preferred not to answer. She'd only recently gotten her father out of her personal business. There was no good reason to get his nose in it again.

Besides today was the day she fixed things. Liv prayed she didn't mess this up. She loved Sam. And Sam loved her. She knew he did. All she had to do was convince him that she wouldn't break his heart this time.

Gus Morgan stepped out onto the porch of the main house as she rolled down her window and turned off the engine. He lumbered down the steps and walked up to the truck, pushing back his Stetson with a finger.

"Miss Olivia. What brings you to the Lazy M?"

"I'm looking for Sam."

His eyes rounded. "I believe he's at home."

"Can you direct me to his house?"

"Sure. You know the road that goes to Drew's house?"

"I do."

"Halfway there, you'll see another road on your right. Take that to Sam's place. Can't miss it. It follows the fence line. He's got a good view of the east pasture from his house."

"Thank you, Gus."

"Everything okay?" he asked. His blue eyes, so much like Sam's, seemed to search her face.

"It will be." She'd do everything she could to make things right with Sam.

"You might want to take a big stick with you," Gus said. "He's been crankier than a bear in a trap."

"I brought his favorite cookies. Ricotta with sprinkles."

"That'll work too," Gus said. He looked at her and seemed to hesitate.

"Was there something else?" Was she imagining things, or did Gus look nervous? He cleared his throat a few times, glanced away and then met her gaze.

"Don't suppose he mentioned that news article to you?"

She swallowed. "We discussed the article last weekend when it came out. Why?"

"I have to make things right with you, Miss Olivia." He kicked at the ground with the toe of his boot. "I was the one who talked to that reporter about Sam. I never imagined things were going to explode because of it. I'm sure sorry to have caused you any trouble."

Liv stared at Gus, her jaw sagging with relief.

"It's okay, Gus. That article didn't explode anything. In many ways, it set things right."

"You're not mad at me then?"

"Not at all, but I appreciate that you solved that puzzle for me."

"Just know that I'm rooting for you, Miss Olivia."

"Thank you." Liv grinned as she started down the road. Gus, not Sam, had tipped off the reporter. She'd jumped to conclusions about him.

That certainly would make today's mission a tiny bit more difficult. But she was an old hand at dealing with impossible situations. She and Sam had a future together and she trusted the good Lord and lots of groveling to make things right.

She followed the directions and turned right halfway to Drew and Sadie's place. About a mile down the road, a house came into view at the top of a small rise—a white ranch house with a wraparound porch.

Liv gasped and hit the brakes. She put a hand to the dash as she flung forward and then back against the seat.

It was the house of her dreams. Liv sat in the truck for minutes, her heart pounding and her hands trembling as they rested on the steering wheel. She took it all in, the red, double front door, the black shutters that framed tall windows, and the cookie-cutter trim on the dormers.

Maybe she was hallucinating. Liv closed her eyes and opened them. The house was still there.

Sam had built her house.

She drove up the drive and parked, grabbed the cookies and got out. It still seemed like she had to be dreaming as she climbed the steps to the porch.

Two shiny black rockers sat on the right with a table between them. Sam had talked about his rocker. To the left, a porch swing moved in the breeze. And there was a breeze. The house was perfectly situated on a small hill that caught the wind and provided an unobstructed view of the pasture.

Unable to resist, she put the cookies on the table and sat on a rocker. She set it in motion and took in the view. Ahead of her, the vista was everything Sam had said it would be. The sun had barely begun to consider setting, creating a backdrop that only the good Lord could have painted. In the distance, a small orchard rose up; beyond that, she could see the roof of Drew and Sadie's house.

She sighed as a roller coaster of emotions rolled through her—delight, joy, and finally, sadness. A deep ache filled her chest, and she rubbed the spot with the heel of her hand, biting back tears.

Sam had built this house for her; she could have been sitting on this porch all along. Then she gave herself grace. *It's okay, Liv. It's your journey, and you're finally here. Home. Where you belong.*

She got up and knocked on the door, but there was no response. Liv turned and walked around the entire porch. Then she spotted Sam, tall and formidable in the distance. He stood at the fence, watching the cattle.

Liv started down the path next to the barbed-wire-and-wood fence. As she got closer, Sam turned around. At first, surprise flickered in the blue eyes. Then the shutters dropped.

He looped his thumbs in his pockets, leaned against a fence post and watched her approach. Today he looked like a cowboy. He hadn't shaved and wore a denim shirt, Wranglers and a black Stetson. His dark hair had grown longer since she'd arrived in May. Maybe because she'd taken up all of his time, as had his woodworking.

You could take the cowboy off the ranch, but you couldn't take the ranch out of the cowboy. She wouldn't have it any other way.

Liv kept walking, finally stopping in front of him. "Nice view."

For moments, he didn't say a word. No, he wouldn't make this easy for her.

"What are you doing here, Liv?" His voice was grim.

"I want to talk."

A bitter smile touched his lips. "I think we're long past talking."

"No. We aren't. I told you before. Our problem is that we don't do enough talking. Besides that, I didn't drive all the way out here on a Sunday to have you shut me out again." Liv stood her ground, despite the pained expression that crossed his face. "We need to finish this once and for all."

Liv didn't miss the irony of the situation. Five years ago she'd left without a word, now she was insisting upon communication. She stared at his face, hard and unyielding today. The blue eyes icy.

"Go ahead," he said. "Clearly, there's no stopping you."

"I'm here to ask your forgiveness for the assumptions I made about you five years ago. For leaving without talking to you."

"Liv, I told you. I forgave you a long time ago. I don't want to think about the past anymore."

"I'm also here to apologize for believing you were responsible for that newspaper article."

He shrugged. "Doesn't really matter, does it?"

"The other reason I'm here is to tell you that The Inspired Kitchen is relocating."

His eyes widened. Yes, that got his attention.

"I've moved my office and the storeroom to the second floor of the restaurant. It was wasted space."

"Wait... You're not relocating away from Homestead Pass?"

Liv frowned. "No. Of course not. I hired a contractor to knock down a wall, and now I have a brand-new shop focusing only on kitchenware."

"You knocked down a wall without asking your landlord?"

"How about that?" She grinned. "The Inspired Kitchen is now accessible from the courtyard. It's perfect."

He looked at her with concern. "What about the store?"

"Obviously, our arrangement has ended. You won the bargain fair and square. I should have given you back your shop when you asked me to in May. There may have been a little pride going on there, on both sides." She released a breath. "Now it's yours. You need more space for your crafts, and I'm hoping this will persuade you to give up at least one of your other jobs to pursue your dream."

"Why are you doing this?" he asked.

"Because it's the right thing to do. I got my dream, and I want you to have yours. I don't want any more bargains, Sam." She hesitated. "By the way, that news article is making its rounds. I heard it even appeared in the Oklahoma City paper. We've got another list of special orders for you."

"That newspaper article." He paused and looked at her. "As long as we're clearing the air, I want to state for the record that I did *not* talk to that reporter."

"I overreacted. I seem to have a habit of doing that. All this time I thought my father was the family drama queen. Turns out I'm guilty too."

Sam tipped back his hat and rubbed his forehead. "Okay. Great. Now, I'm going to have to ask you to stop taking special orders."

"It's not my fault you're so popular. The good news is that things should slow down once we hit Labor Day. We can both catch our breaths then." She kept smiling.

"So that's why you're here?"

"I'm here because I've made so many mistakes. I'm sorry, Sam. For everything." She clasped her hands together tightly as she looked up at him. " I want another chance, and I'm willing to wait around for as long as it takes for that to happen."

"So you want to go back to the way things were? Is that what you're saying?"

"Oh no. I'm exercising my right to a happy ending. I love you, Sam. I love you the way you deserve to be loved. Completely."

Liv swallowed, her heart beating fast as she tried to tell him everything she felt inside. "I don't deserve you, but I love you. Thank you for being the man I need. The man I want." She paused and took a breath. "You always were. I just didn't realize it."

She reached into her pocket and pulled out a small box and flipped open the lid. Nestled inside was an identical ring to the one he had given her and then tossed in Homestead Pass Lake, along with matching bands. His and hers.

Sam stared at her. He opened his mouth and then closed it. She'd apparently shocked him. Well, that was a good sign.

"You don't have to ask me to marry you again. I'm asking you." She fiddled with the box and swiped at the moisture on her face. "When you're ready. I'll be here. Homestead Pass is my forever home."

Sam closed the distance between them

and cupped her face in his hands. "Why are you crying?" he asked, his voice husky.

"Because I caused you so much pain."

He pulled a bandana from his pocket and tenderly wiped her tears. Then he took the ring box from her hand and slipped the engagement ring on her finger. Olivia's heart kept knocking in her chest.

"I love you, Olivia Moretti. Always have. Always will."

She swiped at her eyes. "You built me a house, Sam. Who does that?"

"A man who wants a future with the only woman he's ever loved."

"Oh, Sam," she breathed.

His lips met hers, and she lost herself in his kisses.

"I love happy endings," she said after Sam had kissed her thoroughly.

"Me too." Sam smiled and released a deep sigh of contentment.

"My father will be thrilled that the son he never had will be joining the family in an official capacity."

"Yeah, I guess I get a two-for-one."

Liv laughed. "Please. Don't ever tell him

that." She took his hand and tugged him down the road. "Come on. I want to see my house."

"Yes, ma'am."

Epilogue

Sam stood and clinked his knife against
his water goblet. "May I have your attention?"

The chatter in Liv's restaurant began to
die down.

Liv's gaze spanned the room. Her heart
overflowed at the sight of friends and family gathered in her establishment for the
wedding reception. Amber linens covered
tables adorned with centerpieces of mums
and daisies in fall colors. Pillar candles lit
the room, and a million tiny yellow lights
glowed from the ceiling. The effect was
nothing less than enchanting.

She was so proud of her staff for the

flawless execution of the sit-down dinner. Robyn had returned from Boston for the event and had taken over executive chef duties. Loretta had stepped into the sous-chef role.

Liv focused on Sam as the room became silent. He looked around, his gaze landing on her. She bit back emotion, finding it hard to breathe as the blue eyes overflowing with love pinned her.

"It's not often that we get a second chance at happiness, but today we're thrilled to share exactly that with Anthony and Eleanor," Sam continued. "A toast to the bride and groom, and a thank-you to the good Lord with whom all things are possible. Amen."

"Amen" echoed around the room, followed by an eruption of applause, hoots and whistles. Liv couldn't help but notice that the hoots were mostly from her aunt and Gus Morgan.

A beaming Anthony leaned over to kiss his bride. Eleanor, radiant in a peach lace dress, smiled and touched her husband's cheek tenderly.

It was a bittersweet moment. Liv missed her mother, and yet, there was no doubt in her mind that her dear mamma would approve. She wiped away a tear of pure happiness.

The soft chatter of friendly conversation hummed throughout the room along with the clink of silverware as meals were eaten. In the background, Dean Martin crooned over the DJ's speakers, while a few guests sang along. *"That's amore"* echoed at the song's chorus.

Liv slipped into the kitchen to check on desserts. The cakes waited on a cart, which Loretta would roll into the dining room soon.

A sugar-free lemon cake topped with glazed strawberries for the bride and groom. Next to it, for their guests, sat a traditional, three-layer vanilla cake layered with strawberry preserves and fresh strawberries, topped with vanilla buttercream.

"I wondered where you disappeared to."

Liv turned at Sam's voice and smiled tenderly. How she loved this man who supported her at every turn.

"Everything is perfect, Liv. Your father's face is going to be sore tomorrow from all the grinning he's doing today."

She chuckled. "He took me aside and said becoming a chef was the best decision I ever made, next to agreeing to marry you."

"He's not wrong," Sam said.

"This has been a wonderful day," Liv said. "So much love and support for my father and Eleanor. I adore this town."

Sam nodded. "Me too."

"Come with me." Liv took his hand and led him outside to the patio, where a cool autumn breeze set the wind chimes tinkling as they stepped onto the brick pavers.

"I've been thinking," Liv said.

Sam raised his brows, the blue eyes curious. "Uh-oh."

Thankfully, she'd worn two-inch heels today, which made it a little easier to put her arms around Sam's neck and pull his head down for a soft kiss. Her lips lingered on his for a moment, before she stepped back.

"What have you been thinking, my bride-to-be?"

Liv held up her hand and admired her ring. "I'd like to call in that favor."

"What favor?" He tilted his head and looked at her.

"The one you owe me for the decoy dance."

Sam blew a raspberry. "That was months ago," he protested.

"Six months, that's all. It's now October. It's still a legally binding agreement."

The back door of the restaurant opened, and Loretta popped her head out. "Hurry up, you two. It's time to cut the cake."

"We'll be right there, Zia."

The door closed gently behind her, and Liv pulled Sam into the shadows so they wouldn't be interrupted.

"I've decided that I don't want a big wedding in the spring."

"You've changed your mind?" His eyes flashed with concern.

"I'll never change my mind."

"Then, what?"

"Let's get married in the house you built.

Soon. I've waited too long to become Mrs. Sam Morgan. We'll invite our family, have a simple ceremony and a picnic reception. Loretta can cater the event."

"Yes, to all that." He shook his head as if he couldn't believe what he was hearing. "Thank you, Lord," he murmured.

"Olivia, we're waiting," her father called.

"Yes, Papà." She turned to head back to the restaurant, but Sam took her hand and eased her into his arms.

"I love you, Liv," he whispered. "Thank you for hitching your dreams to mine."

Liv sighed and kissed him.

* * * * *